"We only have a few hours together, so let's make them special..."

There wasn't much time for them to be alone.

"When will we see each other again?" Martha asked.

"Sooner than it's been. It was too long, Martha. I left a *toot* with something in it under your bed. I hope you won't be upset with me. I think it will help while we're apart."

"What is it?" She questioned with her eyes as well as her mouth.

"You'll see soon." Paul grinned and looked into her eyes. "Take care."

"*Jah*, you too," she said as he opened the passenger side in the front and climbed in. Martha greeted his driver, Skip, and then stood with her arms crossed as she watched him make a U-turn on the drive and head for the county road. Paul opened his window and waved as they turned. He looked as sad as she felt.

Oh, if only things were different. They had hoped to be planning their wedding by now.

A year seemed like a long, long time away...

June Bryan Belfie has written over twenty-five novels. Her Amish books have been bestsellers and have sold around the world. She lives in Pennsylvania and is familiar with the ways of her Amish neighbors. Mother of five and grandmother of eight, Ms. Belfie enjoys writing clean and wholesome stories for people of all ages.

MARTHA'S FUTURE

June Bryan Belfie

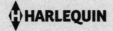

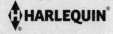

ISBN-13: 978-1-335-49973-8

Martha's Future

Recycling programs
for this product may
not exist in your area.

Copyright © 2017 by June Bryan Belfie

First published in 2017 by June Bryan Belfie. This edition published
in 2020.

This edition published by arrangement with Harlequin Books S.A.

For questions and comments about the quality of this book,
please contact us at CustomerService@Harlequin.com.

Harlequin Enterprises ULC
22 Adelaide St. West, 40th Floor
Toronto, Ontario M5H 4E3, Canada
www.Harlequin.com

Printed in U.S.A.

To my loving husband, Jim,
who continues to encourage me
in my writing addiction.
Thank you, honey.

Chapter One

Martha Troyer and her father sat quietly waiting for Martha's mother to complete her first treatment of radiation for her recently diagnosed breast cancer.

"Do you want me to go down and order *kaffi*?" Martha asked her father, Melvin, who shook his head. He picked up an outdated magazine, which sat on a table next to his chair.

"*Nee*. I've had too much today as it is. It don't help my nerves any."

"*Daed*, *Mamm*'s strong. I think we're more nervous than she is."

"She hides it, is all. I know your *mudder*. She sure hates the thought of leaving us. Not scared for herself. Nope, she's thinking of her family. Always thinking of others."

Martha nodded in agreement. "The nurse said it would be another half hour, so I think I'll go to the cafeteria and have a snack. I was too upset to have breakfast."

"*Jah*, I noticed. Martha, you have to keep up your

strength. We all count on you." He reached into his pocket for money.

"It's okay, *Daed*. I saved a lot while I was working at the restaurant. You keep your money for your own needs."

He nodded and tucked it back in his black trouser pocket. Then he flipped a few pages of the old "Mechanics" magazine and studied an article in an attempt to help pass the time.

Martha took the elevator to the cafeteria where she filled a Styrofoam cup with freshly brewed coffee. She also picked up a blueberry muffin wrapped in plastic wrap. After she paid for them, she made her way to a small table near a window. The cafeteria was about half-filled with visitors and employees of the large hospital facility. She looked around and spotted an Amish woman on the other side of the room. She realized it was one of her own cousins, Lydia. When she caught the young woman's eye, they smiled at each other and nodded, but neither of them rose to join the other.

Later, as Martha was leaving, she stopped to say hello and found out her cousin was waiting for a friend. Lydia pointed to the chair opposite her and Martha sat momentarily to tell her about her mother's condition.

"*Jah*, I just heard about it last week. I'm so sorry, Martha. I'll try to stop by next week to visit with her. I'd have to bring my five little ones, but they behave real *gut*, so it shouldn't be a problem."

"That would be nice, though *Mamm* may be too tired for more company for a while. We have people stop by almost every day since they heard about her cancer. She's still weak from her surgery, and now…"

"*Ach*. Too much company can be difficult. We'll wait then till things are better for you."

Martha smiled broadly. Thankfully, her cousin understood. Then out of the corner of her eye she spotted someone else she knew coming into the large open cafeteria. Daniel Beiler.

"Look," her cousin said, glancing his way. "There's that Daniel who everyone thought you were going to marry. Whatever happened?"

"Oh, it would take too long to tell you the whole story."

"He's grinning over at us. Looks like he still has eyes for a certain Amish girl, and it ain't me," she added patting her expanding belly, confirming Martha's guess that she was expecting yet again.

"Oh dear," Martha said softly as he headed for their table.

"Hello, ladies."

"What are you doing here?" Martha asked, rather curtly.

"I have a doctor's appointment. Just a check-up. And you?"

"*Mamm* is getting radiation."

"Oh, I'm sorry. I thought they'd wait awhile since she just had surgery last week. Is she ready for more treatment?"

"She seems to be. She's very strong, in spite of her condition."

"*Jah*, just like her *dochder*," he said with a grin.

"Stronger than me, I think," Martha said.

"My friend should be waiting for me in her buggy by now," Lydia said as she rose. "I have to get home. My *mudder* is watching my *kinner* and she's got her clothes to hang. Nice to see you both. Here, why don't you sit here, Daniel, and chat a bit with my cousin."

Martha and Daniel looked at each other and then he sat down across from Martha, who shook her head as Lydia walked away. "I must get back. *Mamm* should be finished by now." She stood up abruptly and reached for her shawl.

"I just have one question for you, Martha."

Her brows rose as she stood waiting. "Go on."

"I wondered how things were going with that Paul fellow. I never see him around anymore. Has he cooled off?"

"Not at all. He's just real busy. He's working hard so he can get our home all fixed up before the marriage."

His lips were drawn. It obviously wasn't the answer he had hoped for. "So, it's still on? For the fall?"

"Well, probably not this fall. Not with my *mamm* needing me the way she does. But next fall, that's for sure."

"I see. Well, I'm happy for you—if that's what you want. I guess it will be pretty hard on your parents—you living so far. Since you're their only child…"

"I can visit often."

"Sure. And I know you would, until it got too hard with a whole bunch of *kinner* to think about. Since I know I don't have a chance anymore, I'd still like to be a friend, if you think that would be all right with your future husband."

"Jah, we can be friends. Not close friends, but friends, nevertheless."

"That's all I'm asking, Martha, though I wish it could be more. I'll never be completely over you. That's for certain."

He looked so sad, she actually felt sorry for him. "I hope you find someone else, Daniel. I thought you were seeing Molly Zook now."

"Oh, we go to the sings sometimes, but it's not serious."

"Yet."

"Maybe never. Time will tell. I'm still going out once in a while with an English girl I met, too. Nice girl. Beautiful, but not much up here," he said, pointing to his head.

Martha looked up at his wavy blonde hair. *Jah*, he was still a very attractive man, even though not as handsome as Paul. She'd actually thought she was in love with him at one point. Strange how thoughts and events can change so rapidly in life.

After they parted, she made her way back to the waiting room where her mother was already seated next to her father. "Where have you been?" her father asked, annoyed at her lengthy disappearance.

"I'm sorry. I met a couple people I know. We got to talking. Have you been waiting long?"

"Nee," her mother answered. "Only a couple minutes. Don't be harsh with Martha," she added, turning to her husband. "She has so little time to herself because of me. I sure don't mind waiting ten minutes or so for her."

"I just want to get you home," her husband said, looking chagrined at her rebuke.

"I'll go get the buggy," Martha said quickly. "You take your time and I'll meet you around front."

"Nee, we'd better not bring the buggy around front. Too much traffic," her father said.

"I'm fine to walk. Mercy, don't treat me like a *boppli*." Sarah rose and straightened her back. "It wasn't too bad. Everyone is so nice to me here. They treat me just fine."

"At least that's *gut*," Melvin said, reaching for his wife's arm. "You're going home and resting. Martha will do the cooking today."

"I wish I was better at cooking," Martha said as she walked behind her parents. Once outside, they walked slowly together to the back of the building where there were five other buggies parked in the special spaces provided for the Amish.

"Why that looks like the Beiler's buggy," Sarah stated. "I can tell by that funny stripe on the side. I'm surprised their bishop hasn't mentioned removing it. It sure looks modern."

"The young people get away with such things lately," Melvin said, looking none too happy about the state of affairs with the youth of his community.

"It's yellow to show up at night," Martha explained, as they climbed into their vehicle.

"Did you see any of the Beilers?" her mother asked.

"Just Daniel. He asked how you were doing."

"Such a nice young man. So polite," her mother said, gazing straight ahead.

"He sure weren't polite the day he and Paul Yoder got into it," her father said with a grimace.

"Please. Let's not talk about that," Martha said, remembering all too well the horrors of their confrontation—when the two young men actually got into blows—all over their interest in her. My, what a nightmare!

"That's right," Sarah said, nodding. "But they've both gone before their congregations to ask forgiveness. *Gott*'s forgiven. Can we do less? I see a big difference in Daniel. Look how often he stops by to check on me," she continued.

Melvin rolled his eyes and upon seeing him, Martha let out a giggle.

"You think it's you he's interested in?" he asked his wife. "My, my. Amazes me sometimes. Women can be so *ferndoodled.*"

Martha exchanged looks with her mother. *Men!*

During the rest of the ride, they remained silent, and when they arrived back at their clapboard farmhouse, which was set back off a narrow country road, Sarah allowed her husband to help her up the stairs to her bedroom. She spent the remainder of the afternoon resting.

Martha took out her mother's recipe box and looked for the meatloaf recipe. She was determined to become a really good cook—if it killed her. It was important to be even a better cook than Paul's past girlfriend, Hazel Miller. It hadn't helped Martha's disposition to have Paul remark about Hazel's ability to make amazing meals! Not one bit! Maybe Paul was right when he said he thought she was jealous of Hazel. She really didn't have a right to be upset with him for talking to the girl. After all, Hazel was seeing Paul's partner in his business now, and it seemed to be getting serious. Besides, Paul still loved Martha—that was for sure.

It was true that he hadn't been to see her in a while, but his business was thriving and it demanded a lot of his time, which was a good thing; plus, Martha was needed at home during this difficult time for her dear mother—and her dad, who was busy in his own rights, planting and caring for his animals.

Daniel was her friend, after all, and she had set him

straight today about his chances of being anything more, so Paul would have nothing to be jealous about—or so she thought—though his words and actions of late rather disproved that conclusion.

Oh my, why did life have to be so complicated? Martha added two eggs to the ground venison and then went to the cupboard for breadcrumbs and spices as she tried to concentrate on the meatloaf.

As she squeezed everything together with her clean hands, she heard her mother call down for her. "I'll be up in a minute, *Mamm*. My hands are all gooky."

She formed the loaf in a pan and then washed her hands in hot sudsy water before going up to check on her mother's needs.

When she got upstairs, her mother was coming out of the bathroom. "I'm sick to my stomach already. I can't believe it. I just got the radiation. Years ago, when I had cancer, radiation wasn't nice, but I never *kutzed* from it." There were tears in her eyes, and her skin was pallid.

Martha led her back to her bedroom and helped her back to bed. "I'm so sorry, *Mamm*. I'll get a cool washcloth to lay on your head. Maybe part of it is because you're pretty upset. You haven't eaten all day, either. I'll bring you a cup of tea and some crackers."

Sarah patted her daughter's hand. "You're so *gut* to me. What would I ever do without you?"

Martha kissed her cheek and left the room before she, too, would be shedding tears. Indeed. What would her parents do without her?

Chapter Two

Paul and Jeremiah, his partner in the carpentry business, stopped for a coffee break after loading the truck with the cabinetry they'd completed for the model home. They'd finished building them, but now they'd spend at least a full day installing them in the new house. They'd made the deadline, and it was time to relax for a few minutes to enjoy their success. If the builder was satisfied, there'd be more jobs ahead. Big ones.

Ben, their new Mennonite carpenter, came in from the truck where he'd been covering the cabinets with tarps to protect them for the half-hour drive. He had a *toot*—or bag—of fresh donuts to contribute. "Fresh from the oven. I stopped at my sister's house on the way over. I know she always fries up donuts on Mondays. Wait till you try them."

"Can't be as *gut* as Hazel's," Jeremiah bragged.

"*Jah*, she makes the best," Paul confirmed.

"Another reason I'm surprised you broke off with her," Jeremiah noted as he reached in the bag for one of the warm donuts.

"Well, there are other things besides being a *gut* cook, you know," Paul said with a grin.

"Anyway, I'm glad you did break up, because I think she just may be the one for me."

"And my Martha is the *maed* for me," Paul said with a huge grin. "Just wish things were different with her family situation. It doesn't look like we'll be marrying for a while."

Ben looked over at his friend as he broke off half of a second donut. "Because of her mother's cancer?"

"*Jah*, that's the main thing right now. I think I told you that Martha was adopted, right?"

Ben and Jeremiah nodded.

"They'd kept that a secret from her all her life. They're lucky she didn't have a problem when she found out. Some *maedel* would have been upset."

"I thought Martha was upset," Jeremiah said.

"Not for long. She was upset no one trusted her enough to tell her sooner, but she seemed to understand her *mudder*'s reason for the secrecy. Anyway, I think Martha's even more devoted to them now. I'm not sure she'll ever be ready to move away. It scares me."

"Oh, after her mother's better, I'm sure she'll come around," Ben said, as he reached for the coffee pot and poured everyone a second cup.

"I sure hope so. It puts a strain on us."

"Once this project is complete," Jeremiah said, looking over at Paul, "why not take a couple days off and go see Martha. I'm sure that would help."

"Think it would be okay?"

"You have a life beyond carpentry, *jah*?"

Paul nodded, as a smile spread across his face. "I'll

do that and I'll surprise her. Do you think we'll be done by Tuesday?"

"Should be, though it might be safer to make it Wednesday."

"I'll stop by Skip Davis's house on the way home and set something up for the drive. I think that's what we both need. Some time together alone."

"I'm glad I live near my *maed*," Jeremiah said. "I don't think being apart is such a *gut* idea. Too bad you can't marry this fall."

Paul nodded in agreement and reached for another donut. "This is *gut*, but I think Hazel's are better," he added.

When they were done, they got into the truck and drove to the model home to set up. Paul whistled all the way, at least until the other two threatened to leave him off in the woods.

Since Lizzy was headed to her sister's house to visit with their parents for a few hours, she took the photograph of Martha's birth father with her. Her mother had never seen the picture. Lizzy wouldn't show the photograph to her sister with all she was going through, but her mother had expressed an interest in seeing it.

Sarah's radiation treatments were scheduled weekdays for several weeks. Lizzy couldn't remember how long they were to last, but the doctor had mentioned starting chemo once the radiation was complete. Her poor sister. She had not done well with chemo years before when she was previously treated for cancer, but it had done the job and kept her cancer-free for all these years. Hopefully, she'd be able to conquer this latest attack. Her sister was strong and determined, but she was that much older now, and everything seemed more difficult as one aged.

Lizzy decided to make an appointment to check out her recurrent neck pain. She knew she had some arthritis in her cervical spine area, but it had worsened considerably as of late. She noticed it especially when she tried to quilt. Would her dear niece's quilt ever be completed at the rate the three ladies were going? Well, apparently the wedding wouldn't take place for at least a year now, so they had plenty of time to worry about it.

Worry, she did, but not about the quilt so much. No, her concern—after her main problem of her sister's cancer was addressed—was the fact that Martha was overly solicitous toward her mother to the point of being unhealthy—at least in her humble opinion. She didn't talk about Paul much, now that she was home. Goodness, it would be terrible if she ended up breaking off with Paul because of Sarah's health issues. Lizzy knew of a young girl who gave up her chance to marry just to stay at home and help with her younger brother, who had mild Down syndrome. It was very sweet of her, but now she was in her fifties and her beau had long since married her best friend, and they were now parents of eleven children. Actually, maybe the girl had made the right decision! That was quite a passel of *kinner*!

Lizzy poured herself a glass of orange juice and sat down at the kitchen table, the envelope with the photo in her hand. She removed it and examined every detail of the handsome young Italian man, who had stolen the heart of a young Amish woman twenty-plus years ago. His smile reminded her of her niece's smile. It lit up his face and his dark eyes twinkled as he waved to the photographer.

As she looked at the photo, her husband, Leroy Fisher, came through the kitchen doorway and washed his hands over at the sink. "I'm quitting for the day. Got what I wanted done and so I'm going to spend some time with you. Whatcha looking at, Liz?"

"Martha's father."

"What was his name again?" he asked as he reached for a terry towel.

She flipped the photograph over and read the neatly written name. "Alexandro Gionnardo."

"That's a hard one to remember."

"*Jah.* He was sure a *gut*-looking young man."

Leroy sat down across from her as she handed it over to him.

"Took advantage of that poor young *maed.*"

"Jah, Rosie Esh was her name. She looked so woebegone when she showed up with her *boppli.*"

"Sure. She was upset. It's a big thing to give up your own baby for adoption. Have to hand it to her. It was the right thing for the *maed*, especially since the young man was back in Italy."

"I don't think she ever told him about Martha. Maybe she didn't have his address," Lizzy said. She clucked her tongue, reached for the picture and tucked it back in the yellowish envelope.

"So, what are you going to do with it?"

"I want to get it to Martha somehow, but it might upset my *schwester* to know we even have it. In the meantime, maybe my *mudder* will keep it."

"Why don't you wait awhile. What's the rush? Martha's waited this long. What's another month or so. Wait till Sarah is doing better."

"I guess you're right. I just feel a little guilty hanging on to it when I know how much it would mean to Martha to have it."

"Has she asked you for it?"

"Not really. You're right. Now is not the time. I'll put it back in my desk, but if anything happens…"

"Don't talk foolishness. You're the healthiest one in the family. You ain't going anywhere for a long time."

"Leroy, you know no one knows the future. Only *Gott* knows. I just want to tell you where to find it."

"Okay, I got it. Now what do you have hidden in the cookie jar? I smelled something *gut* coming from the oven when I came in before."

She laughed and patted his hand. "I made molasses cookies, one of your favorites."

"Must be my birthday, I guess," he teased.

"As a matter of fact, it's our anniversary. Thirty-eight years of marriage to the same man. Can you believe it?"

"Hey, I'm married to a *grossmammi*. A young lookin' farmer like me." He lifted her hand to his lips. "And I'm mighty glad we found each other. I had a crush on you when I was ten."

"I know, I know. I've heard it a million times. And when I looked at you and smiled, you near passed out. Silly *bu*."

There was never a celebration on their anniversary, but when they hit fifty, she planned to throw a great big party for everyone she knew. That was something to look forward to.

Chapter Three

The next day, Sarah did better with her treatment. She was tired when she returned home, but her stomach didn't give her any issues, and she figured it had been nerves the day before, on top of not eating, which had caused her upset. After resting for about an hour, as she and Martha worked in the kitchen towards supper, they heard a buggy grind its way over their stone driveway. A few minutes later, Daniel Beiler appeared at the kitchen door window, beaming through the glass. Martha smiled back as she opened the door and invited him in.

"*Hallo*, ladies." He removed his straw hat and stood twisting the brim in his hands.

"Well, seat yourself down," Sarah said, "and I'll make a pot of *kaffi*."

"*Nee*, that's okay. I'm headed home. I just wanted to see how you were doing."

"Not too bad today. Sit for a minute. Martha, get the young man some of those molasses cookies your *aenti* brought over."

Martha put the potato peeler aside and obeyed her

mother. She set a plate in front of him with four cookies and asked if he wanted a glass of milk.

"*Jah*, sure. Sounds *gut*. And how are you doing, Martha?"

"Same as always. As long as *Mamm* is doing *gut*, I'm
in fine spirits." She smiled over at Sarah, who grinned
back.

"How was your work today?" Martha asked him.

"I've been working the fields with my *daed* all day.
But I showered before coming by. With all the rain
we've had, my boots sure were a muddy mess by the
end of the day."

"Oh, ain't that the truth?" Sarah said, clucking her
tongue. "Melvin takes a *gut* hour cleaning up every
night."

"You still like farming though?" Martha asked.

"*Jah*, I guess so. I love being on the land. Can't imagine being in a building all day doing carpentry or fac-
tory work."

"Paul loves his carpentry," Martha stated as she returned to her job peeling potatoes.

"*Jah*, I'm sure he'd never want to leave his job. Too
bad it's so far from your folks."

"Only a couple hours," Martha noted.

"By car though, right?"

"*Jah*." She frowned as she realized what he was
doing. Always getting little digs in.

"Have you thought about getting your own land?"
Sarah asked, as she stood at one of the counters by the
sink and continued the job of slicing a cabbage for slaw.

"Someday I will. I'm waiting for the land next to my
daed's to come up for sale. The owner never comes by.
He's from out of town, you know."

"*Jah*, an Englisher, I've heard. Why does he keep it?"

"Don't know. Maybe wants to sell it to a builder and make himself a lot of money, but I'm hoping he'll be ready to sell when I'm ready to buy. I'm saving my money now."

"*Jah*, you'll want a family one of these days," Sarah said without looking over at her daughter, who remained silent as she took her time removing the skin from the potatoes.

Daniel replied without hesitation. "And I know just who I want to be my wife."

"Well now, ain't that nice. Do you want to share the news?" Sarah looked over and grinned.

"Sorry, but that's a secret for now."

Martha couldn't stay silent any longer. "I bet she's a redhead."

"Nope."

"Well, *gut* luck with her, Daniel. I hope she'll love you as much as I love my Paul."

His eyes met hers briefly and she realized she'd probably gone too far. His look of disappointment actually touched her heart—momentarily.

Daniel reached for another cookie and chewed in silence. Then he rose and said his good-byes. "I'll stop by soon again, Mrs. Troyer. Keep strong."

"*Jah, danki.* Stop anytime, Daniel, and say *hallo* to your family for us."

He nodded and closed the door behind him. Martha peeked out the kitchen window and watched as he walked slowly towards his parked buggy. She shouldn't have been so unkind in her response, but she certainly didn't want to encourage the man, and she knew he had not yet given up hope. Next time, she'd try to be a little nicer. He did seem to be different. Maybe he was remorseful over his earlier behavior. She'd once found him to be a potential partner—before Paul came into her life.

Martha decided to spend some time the next morning with her grandparents, before going for radiation with her mother. She hadn't helped her grandmother clean for several days and the last time she'd scrubbed their small bathroom and kitchen floors, she'd found cobwebs forming in the corners.

When she went into the living room, her grandfather was reading his Bible while rocking in his favorite chair. She was shocked by his appearance. His hair, usually tidy and combed back, was bedraggled and looked in the need of a shampoo. Even his clothes looked somewhat shabby. He'd always had good grooming and it alarmed her. Had her grandmother not noticed?

Martha went over to her grandfather and patted his shoulder. Then she leaned over and kissed his cheek, though she didn't breathe—just in case.

Mammi Nancy came into the living room and greeted Martha with a gentle hug. "You're here bright and early. Everything okay at home?"

"Oh, fine. Well, as *gut* as can be expected. I just thought I'd scrub down your floors this morning before we leave for the treatment. Is now a *gut* time?"

"As *gut* a time as any. Let me sweep up first."

"I'll do it, *Mammi*, but you can keep me company while I sweep."

The two women went into the kitchen and after taking the broom and dustpan from the broom closet, Martha laid them aside temporarily and whispered in her *mammi*'s ear. "Is *Dawdi* sick?"

Nancy looked somewhat alarmed at the question. "Why? Does he look that bad?"

"He's awful pale and his hair's a mess. That's not like him."

"*Jah*, he doesn't seem to care much what he looks like. He spends more and more time in bed, too. I'm surprised he's still sitting there. He's been there since breakfast."

"Why won't he see his doctor? Maybe something is wrong?" Martha asked, keeping her voice low.

"I've told him too many times. I get tired of trying. Even your *mudder* has tried. Men can be stubborn, you know."

Martha smiled. "*Mamm* says the same thing. I hope Paul isn't this stubborn."

"Oh, he will be as he gets older," Nancy said with a half grin. "Just keep loving him anyway."

"That's for certain," Martha said. She then began her project while her grandmother wiped down the counters and cabinet doors.

As Martha finished up the kitchen floor, still kneeling on a folded towel to get into the corners, she heard someone at the back door. When she looked over at the visitor who was coming in, she gasped. "Oh, my goodness! It's Paul!"

She dropped the sponge in the pail of sudsy water and managed to rise without toppling over. When she got to the door and opened it, Paul stood before her, grinning widely.

"*Jah*, it's me all right. Here to see my sweetheart." He reached for her hands and helped her to steady herself.

Mammi had slipped out of the room and Martha could hear her talking in the front room with her husband.

Quickly, they took advantage of their moment alone, and kissed briefly on the lips. Then Martha stood back, still holding on to his hands. "Why didn't you let me know?"

"You don't have a cell phone and I just decided a couple days ago. Besides, I wanted to surprise you. I've missed you so much." He drew her into his arms and caressed her back. "Did you miss me?"

"More than you'll ever know. I'm sorry I didn't call you last night. I'm just so tired sometimes…"

"It's okay. I understand. We've been real busy ourselves, as you know."

"What about your kitchen project?"

"Done. We finished installing it yesterday, so Jeremiah suggested I take a day off."

"Oh, I thought you were partners. Couldn't you have decided for yourself?"

"Sure, but it's better if he suggests it. Don't forget, it was his business first. I don't want to upset him."

"*Jah*, I see." *She didn't.* "Are you hungry? Can I fry up eggs for you?"

"*Nee*, I'm fine."

"What time do you have to leave?"

"Not until seven tonight. We have all day to be together."

"Well almost. I go with my mother for her radiation treatments. She counts on me being there."

"That's okay. Can I go with you?"

"Sure. We can wait in the waiting room together. It takes a while, but at least we'll be able to talk and catch up."

"Who else goes? Your *daed*?"

"*Jah*, but with you there, maybe he'll stay back and get some work done. It's hard on him, too."

"I'm sure it is. I'd be real upset if my wife had cancer. Who wouldn't be?"

"*Jah*. I wonder what my genes hold," Martha said thoughtfully.

"Maybe someday you'll find out more."

"Hopefully. I was going to look into it, but that was before all this happened. It's on a back burner, as my English friends say."

"You look wonderful, though I think you've lost some weight," Paul said as he stood back, still holding her hands in his.

"Maybe a little. I don't know. I don't weigh myself, but my *fracks* are a little looser."

"You have to keep up your strength—for your *mudder*'s sake as well as your own," he added.

"You sound more like my *daed* than my boyfriend," she teased.

"I'm just concerned."

She heard her grandmother returning and removed her hands from his. "Let me clean up and we can go for a walk. You saw my folks already?"

"*Jah*, I stopped there first. Your *mamm* looks pretty *gut*, considering."

"She does. She's strong, Paul. I hope I'd be as strong."

"You would be, Martha. You have *Gott* to give you what you need."

"True, and He's been faithful about giving me enough strength through all this."

After they said good-bye to her grandparents, they walked over to the pasture where some of the cows were grazing. Millie, their oldest and most faithful cow, came over to be patted on the head. "Look, she always knows me," Martha said, pleased with the attention.

"She's doing better now?" he asked.

"Oh, *jah*. My *daed* treats her special."

"How long are these treatments going to go on with your *mudder*?" he asked, leaning against the fence.

"About six more weeks and then they'll start chemo. That's when it gets harder on *mamm*."

"What a shame. But if it heals her, it's worth it."

"It has to. I don't know what I'd do without my *mamm*. She's always been there for me." Millie trudged away and Martha turned to face Paul.

"You have me, Martha. You'll always have me beside you."

She leaned against him and felt his arms surround her. "*Jah*. Thank goodness. I wish we were married."

"That makes two of us. When do you—"

"Don't even ask. I have no idea. First things first, Paul. Once *Mamm* is all better, then we can make our plans."

"Honey, that might be a year," he said.

"Whatever it is—it is. We can't think of ourselves at a time like this."

He let a long breath escape, but didn't say a word. They remained embraced for several minutes. Then she stepped back. "Tell me about the house. Have you finished painting?"

"Not really. I've been too busy to work on it. Besides, there's no rush now. I did move in last week though. I was going to wait, but it's much easier being right there. That way I can work the evenings, too."

"Things will slow down a little now that the model kitchen is done, won't they?"

"Actually, a new customer came in last week and wants us to build a wall of cabinets and shelves for his library. And of course, he wants it right away. Ben's working on the plans now. He's got a *gut* head for design. We're lucky to have him."

"And is Jeremiah still going with Hazel?"

"*Jah*, they seem to be pretty cozy."

"That's *gut*," she responded. "I guess now that things are a little slower, she won't have to cook for you anymore."

"Jeremiah's hoping she'll still do it."

"And you?"

"I think that's a trick question," he said, grinning widely.

"Maybe it is," she said sheepishly. "Okay, don't answer. Let's go back to the house. I want to fix dinner so we can eat before we have to go. *Mamm*'s appointment is at three."

"What are you making for dinner?" he asked, taking her hand as they walked slowly towards the farmhouse.

"Pot roast with potatoes and carrots."

"Sounds *gut*. Onions, too?"

"Of course. And I have rolls left from yesterday."

"Dessert?"

"Goodness! Did you come to see me or eat my food?" she asked, grinning over at him.

"Just checking."

"*Mamm* made a huge pot of rice pudding this morning. We have enough for the week."

"Sounds *gut*. Hazel made… Oops! Forget it."

Martha growled over. "You're a tease, Paul Yoder!"

"Yup. I love to see your face when I mention her."

"I see. Well then, two can play that game. Daniel still comes by to check on *mamm*."

Paul's smile dropped. "Oh, I'm sure he's all concerned about your *mudder*. Has nothing to do with her *dochder*, of course."

Now it was Martha's turn to laugh. "Well…" she said coquettishly.

"Let's not talk about him, Martha. Or Hazel. We only have a few hours together, so let's make them special."

"I agree," she said. They stopped walking and she returned to his waiting arms. Then they separated and went into the kitchen to work on dinner.

After a delicious meal, Paul offered to drive their buggy to the hospital. Melvin stayed back in order to catch up on some of his farm work. He seemed grateful to have Paul there, and Sarah encouraged her husband to remain at home. "It's fine, Melvin," she added as she climbed into the back of the family buggy. Melvin stood watching with a grim expression. "Goodness, I have Martha with me, too. Stop looking so sad. We won't be gone long."

Martha sat up front with Paul, while her mother leaned back with her eyes closed. Martha wondered if she was praying or just resting.

She and Paul talked about his business and then he listened as she spoke about her grandparents. When she mentioned her grandfather's pallor and lack of energy, Sarah leaned forward to join in. "We've been trying to get him back to the doctor's. We're concerned as well, Martha. Maybe he needs stronger heart medicine. It's almost like he doesn't care if he gets better or not. Poor *Mamm*. She's so worried about him. It ain't fair.

He needs to take better care of himself—for the family, if not for himself."

"Maybe *Daed* should talk to him," Martha suggested.

"Apparently, he's tried, but *Dawdi* says he's just fine and everyone should let him be."

Paul listened without comment. No sense getting into a family situation. He wanted to keep things as smooth as he could since he was not always in the family's good graces. Right now, things were going pretty well.

There wasn't much time for them to be alone, but while Sarah was having her radiation treatment, they sat and talked about everything on their minds. It was so much easier in person. Oh, if only…

After they arrived back at the house, Martha and Paul took another walk, but Martha insisted on getting back to work on supper and to check on her mother, who was napping after her radiation. Fortunately, she complained only of fatigue. Her hair had not begun to fall out.

Martha planned to eat a little earlier so Paul could stay for supper and not feel rushed. She worked hard to make the kind of coleslaw he liked—with extra mayonnaise. Neither Daniel nor Hazel were mentioned again, and it was a pleasant day.

After the supper, Paul excused himself to use the upstairs bathroom. When he came down, he and Martha waited outside on the front porch for his ride. When they figured they were truly alone, they held hands and Paul sneaked several kisses before the car turned onto the drive and headed up to take him back home.

Martha had a heavy heart as she walked over to the

car with him. "When will we see each other again?" she asked.

"Sooner than it's been. It was too long, Martha. I left a *toot* with something in it, under your bed. I hope you won't be upset with me. I think it will help while we're apart."

"What is it?" She questioned with her eyes as well as her mouth.

"You'll see soon." He grinned and looked into her eyes. "Take care."

"*Jah*, you, too," she said as he opened the passenger side in the front and climbed in. Martha greeted his driver, Skip, and then stood with her arms crossed as she watched him make a U-turn on the drive and head for the county road. Paul opened his window and waved as they turned. He looked as sad as she felt.

Oh, if only things were different. They had hoped to be planning their wedding by now. A year seemed like a long, long time away.

Martha walked back to the house and went in to clean up the kitchen. She decided to make a fruit salad, in case her mother wanted a snack before bedtime. Now, fruit salad was something she made real *gut*. Then she remembered Paul saying he'd left something for her under her bed. She set the bananas aside and went quickly up to her room.

Chapter Four

Rose Esh unzipped her second suitcase and filled the bureau drawers in her room with several knit shirts and jeans. It was a charming country inn outside of Lancaster, reasonably priced and fortunately, available for an entire month. It was convenient being a writer, since you could be anywhere in the world and not be away from your work. Well, anywhere that has electricity, she thought, as she laid her Mac laptop on the long table that would serve as her desk.

With all the traveling she'd done, she'd never been to Lancaster, Pennsylvania. She had attended a writer's conference once in Pittsburgh, but that was at least ten years earlier. The terrain was similar to where she resided. She lived in Oakwood, a lovely suburb of Dayton, in a two-story Colonial, which was free of a mortgage and fairly easy to maintain.

Her husband, Monty, had left her well-fixed when he passed away suddenly after only five years of marriage. He was quite a bit older, and she married him more for security than out of love. They were relatively happy together—never argued—but when she was honest to herself, she admitted preferring the single life now, having complete control and no distractions.

Rose set the empty suitcase under the bed, next to a smaller case she'd brought, and then decided to take a shower before driving into Lancaster for a bite to eat. After she dressed in fresh clothing, she dabbed some make-up over her clear ivory skin and added a squirt of light perfume.

Where to begin. She couldn't find anything online that gave her any information as to the whereabouts of her daughter. She hadn't expected anything, but there was always a chance something would pop up.

As she drove into the center of the city, she found herself checking out every Amish buggy or young woman with plain clothing in the hopes of spotting Martha. Rather foolish, really. What were the chances? Besides, she had no idea what the girl would look like as an adult. Even in Ohio, she couldn't help herself from looking and wondering when she spotted young girls the approximate age as her Martha. As a babe, her daughter had resembled the father with her slightly olive skin and dark, wavy hair. She was not the typical fair-skinned blonde most people envisioned the Amish to look like. No, she wouldn't look anything like her birth mother.

Why, after all these years, was it so important to find her? She had no plans to meet with her. She just wanted to see her—even from afar—to assure herself that the decision made so many years before had been a wise one. At the time, it seemed like the only one, since her parents were ready to pack her bags and send her off alone, if she insisted on raising the child herself.

She knew she'd been wrong to become intimate with a man she wasn't married to, or even intended to marry.

God would not be happy. But they were so in love—and young, and her innocence kept her from weighing the consequences. She'd never wanted any children after that. Perhaps she felt she didn't deserve any. Strange, when she married her husband, they never did anything to prevent her from becoming pregnant, but apparently, it wasn't God's will, since she remained barren.

Not being particularly hungry, she settled for an ice cream shop, which also featured sandwiches on the billboard. She pulled into the lot, entered, and took her seat at a small square table next to a window. The room was half-filled with smiling tourists and local families. After eating a tuna salad sandwich with a chocolate milkshake, she took a walk around the area. Why was she here? What a foolish thing she'd done. The only information she'd been given, was the family had moved to Lancaster County when Martha was about a year old.

Maybe she should just pack up the next day and go into Philadelphia, where she could attend a concert or something stimulating.

She exhaled a long breath and decided against that plan. She'd agreed to do a book signing of her newly published Amish novel in Lancaster, which was scheduled in two weeks. Her agent had been excited when she learned Rose's plan to be in Pennsylvania. Her earlier books were non-fiction and centered around her life as an Amish girl, but now she'd expanded into writing novels. Her pen name was Astrid Flemming. She had thought of using her maiden name, Esh, but wanted to remain anonymous. She still felt shame from her early decisions, which led to her illegitimate child.

A gift shop attracted her attention with their display of faceless Amish dolls and handmade miniature buggies. She walked in and perused the merchandise. One of the clerks was talking to a well-dressed tourist as she rang up the woman's sale. "Oh, yes, I know tons of Amish people," she was saying.

"Are they as strange as they look?" the woman asked as she opened her purse and reached for her wallet.

"They're pretty much like we are, only quiet when they're in public."

"I heard they're rather ignorant. I know they don't believe in education."

Rose couldn't stand by any longer. She walked over. "Sorry to interrupt, but I was Amish myself as a girl, and the Amish are far from ignorant."

The clerk and her customer stared at Rose, but listened attentively.

"They don't need more than an eighth-grade education for the lives they lead," she continued. "They've chosen their lifestyle to avoid the culture we see ourselves living in today. By separating themselves, they can remain true to God and to the moral ways they've chosen."

"If it's so great, why did you leave?" asked the customer.

"For personal reasons, but I'm grateful for the training I received. I went on and got my degree, but that doesn't mean I'm smarter than my friends who remained Amish."

"I didn't mean to offend anyone," the woman said, embarrassed that she had been overheard. "One reason my husband and I came to Lancaster was to learn more about the Amish. I'm glad I met you."

"I've written several books about my early years as an Amish girl. If you give me your name and address,

I'd be happy to send a couple of them to you. I'm sorry I interrupted. It was rude of me."

"No, of course you were offended. I'll just buy your books. What is your name?"

"My pen name is Astrid Flemming, but my maiden name was Rose Esh. I'm having a book signing in two weeks. I'll give you my card."

"Oh, we'll be back in Missouri by then," the woman said, a look of disappointment spreading across her face. "But I'll take your card and order them from my bookstore back home." She extended her hand and Rose reciprocated. They shook hands and Rose handed her the card.

The clerk smiled over. Rose moved away from the counter and returned to her place by the dolls. She remembered playing with one her mother had made, which looked very much like the one for sale. On impulse, she bought it and also purchased two linen dishcloths with colorful illustrations of Amish girls hanging clothes. Cute, though nothing she'd ever considered purchasing in the past.

Once she returned to the inn, she collected the items she'd bought and headed to her room. On the way she met the owner, a sweet middle-aged woman, most likely a Mennonite from the way she was dressed. They greeted each other and then Rose asked if she had a moment to answer a couple questions.

"Of course. Would you care for some tea? I was just going to make a pot. My husband is attending a meeting, so I was going to relax and then work on some sewing I've put off."

"That sounds delightful. I'll leave this package off and join you in a minute."

"Good. The kitchen is straight down the long hallway. You can't miss it."

Rose removed the doll from the bag and laid it against her pillow. Déjà vu. A trip back in time to her small stark bedroom she shared with her sister Ida. What had become of her? And her three brothers? She'd heard her father had passed away about ten years after she left home, but she knew nothing about the rest of the family—her mother included. *Mamm*. She thought very seldom about her past life. Only once had she driven past the old homestead, but there was another name on the mailbox and the old clapboard house had been resided in blue and looked nothing like the home she'd been raised in. It had been a painful journey, and she never returned.

The doll brought a wave of sadness and almost physical pain. Perhaps she'd give it away. She didn't want to be reminded of her past life. But for now…

The dishtowels would remain in her possession. They were cute, but did not bring back memories. Their towels had been plain white. Like everything else. Plain.

She wiped tears, which had surfaced and patted her cheeks with some face powder before heading downstairs. When she got to the kitchen, her hostess, Phyllis, was setting up two cups with matching saucers at the table. She looked up and smiled. "I should have asked what kind of tea you drink, but I figured everyone likes English Breakfast, so that's what I'm brewing."

"You guessed right," Rose said as she took the seat at the side of the table, leaving the end seat for her hostess.

"Have you had a chance to settle in?" Phyllis asked, as she brought a bright red ceramic teapot to the table and set it down on a trivet in the shape of a cow.

"Yes, and it's very homey."

They discussed Ohio, and Rose told her about her writing. Soon she found herself discussing her early days as an Amish girl. Phyllis seemed sincerely interested in her story. Unexpectedly, Rose began telling her new friend about her reason for being in Lancaster. Phyllis did not seem shocked at the disclosure, rather she seemed saddened by the story of the adoption.

"That must have been a difficult time for you, poor girl," she said as she stirred sugar into her cup of tea.

"Yes, it was horrible. I wanted to raise my baby, but there was no way I could manage it without my family's support."

Phyllis nodded. "It happens in our community, too, and it's difficult for everyone concerned. And twenty years ago, it was almost impossible for an unmarried girl to raise her own child. I'm sure you made the right decision at the time. You haven't had any correspondence with the adoptive family?"

"None. That was part of the arrangement. I did meet them though when I surrendered my baby, and I was pleased. My Martha seemed to fit right in. Her new mother, Sarah, was very sweet and loving." Rose stopped speaking for a moment and concentrated on her tea, stirring extra sugar in, slowly. "I've never said those words out loud before. 'New mother.' The thought used to be too painful to even think in those terms, but with the passage of time…"

"Yes, time heals. I lost my mother when I was six. She died in childbirth. I've never fully gotten over it. When I was nine, my father remarried and my stepmother was kind to me and my two sisters, which was a blessing. We're actually still very close."

"I'm glad things worked out for you."

"For three years though, after my mother died, I was an unhappy little girl. My grandparents were good to me, but they were in poor health and didn't spend much time with the family. And my dad had his own grief to deal with."

"Somehow we get through rough times."

"Only with the help of God. He's been my rock."

"And mine," Rose said. She sipped the hot tea, and for a moment neither of them spoke.

"I know a lot of the Amish around here, Rose. What was the family name of the people who adopted your daughter?"

"Troyer. The father was Melvin, and the mother was Sarah," she replied.

"I know a couple Troyer families. No one by the name of Melvin, however. They live over outside of Paradise. You might consider going to the post office and asking about the last name. I don't know if they'd give out any information though."

"I doubt it. The privacy laws would most likely forbid it. I don't know what I expected when I came here with so little information. It was probably a fool's errand."

"No, perhaps God has led you here to find your daughter. If that's the case, you will find her—probably in the least expected way. I'll be praying for you. Let me get some of the cookies my sister brought me yesterday. She bakes all the time." Phyllis got up from the table and brought back a cookie jar loaded with chocolate chip cookies. "Chocolate always helps," she added with a pat on the shoulder and a tender smile. Indeed.

Chapter Five

Martha reached her bedroom and peeked under the bed. A small *toot* had been pushed halfway under. She knelt down and reached for it. What had he left for her? When she opened it, she found a black flip lid cell phone. Oh, goodness, why did he keep pushing phones on her? *Jah*, it would make life simpler, but he knew how much her parents were against their use. When she left in the evenings to use the community phone, her father would frown over at her. Though he never asked where she was going, she suspected he knew. But at least, she didn't own one. Not until now. She tucked it back in the bag and placed it in her dresser drawer under her nightwear. She'd have to think about it. It would definitely be convenient. *Oh,* Gott—*what would you have me do?*

"Martha, would you help me carry food over to *Mammi*'s place?" she heard her mother call up the stairs.

"*Jah*, I'll be right down," she yelled back.

They stayed for about an hour, sitting with her grandparents while they ate their supper. Her grandfather barely spoke and ate only a small portion of the meal.

Before they went back home, *Mammi* spoke quietly to Martha and Sarah when her husband was out of the room. "He's agreed to see a doctor. I'm going to use the community phone tomorrow, if one of you can take me. He's not sleeping *gut* anymore. I think he's worried about his health and won't admit it."

"I'm glad you got him to agree to see his doctor," Sarah said. "I'll drive you tomorrow."

"*Mamm*, you'll have your radiation treatment and may be too tired. I'll drive *Mammi*."

"Well, okay."

Mammi nodded. "That would be better. It's nice to have youth, Martha. Enjoy these years. You're old before you know what happened to all that time."

"I've heard that before, *Mammi*. I try to appreciate every day the Lord gives me, but I do take it for granted sometimes."

"*Jah*," her mother said in agreement. "We take our health for granted as well."

"It's hard not to," Martha said.

"*Jah*, it takes something like cancer to make you stop and think," Sarah said, her tone solemn.

"Are you scared, Sarah?" her mother asked, her lips trembling ever so slightly.

"Maybe a little, *Mamm*, but then I talk to *Gott*, and He makes me calm down."

"I'm glad. I've been talking more to Him lately myself. I try not to question."

"It doesn't get you anywhere," Sarah said. "Just have to trust. That's all we can do."

"So, Martha, things still *gut* with that young man of yours?" her grandmother asked, changing the subject intentionally.

"Pretty *gut, jah*. He's having trouble accepting the fact that our wedding has to be delayed."

Sarah looked stunned. "You don't have to wait, Martha. We can plan for a fall wedding. It's only April. We have plenty of time."

"I couldn't go ahead with a wedding while you're still faced with all this."

"Of course, you can."

"Well, I'm not even baptized."

"Go talk to the bishop."

"*Mamm*, I wouldn't feel right."

"Honey," Sarah started, as she reached for Martha's hands, "if things don't go the way we want them to, I'd be much happier knowing you were taken care of and happy."

"But you need me to help—"

"You're a wonderful help to me and *Daed*, and I appreciate everything you do, but I want you to be with Paul. I see how you love him, and I don't want you to be worrying about us all the time."

"I don't know what to say. You're so unselfish, *Mamm*. That's one of the things I love most about you, but I don't think I could leave you two to go through all this without being here with you. Please let me think about everything first."

"Of course. Now give me a hug, *liebschdi*. You're the joy of my life."

Mammi wiped her eyes. "I'll take a hug while you're giving them out, sweetheart."

After embracing her mother, Martha moved over to her grandmother and held her ever so gently in her arms. At that moment, she was sure her place was here for the foreseeable future. The wedding could wait.

* * *

Paul sat on the edge of his bed the next evening, holding his phone. It continued to ring Martha's cell phone, but there was no answer. Not even an answering service. Apparently, she still felt somehow it was wrong to use a phone. He should have known better. She'd made it clear before that her parents' wishes came first. Yes, it was foolish of him to push it on her. Hopefully, she'd call him later from the community phone and he'd apologize about his "surprise."

He might as well go back to the workshop and finish up the shelving he'd been sanding. Sleep evaded him many nights. Sometimes his guilt kept him awake. Guilt from his annoyance with Martha's apparent refusal to even consider marrying in the fall. She seemed overly concerned about remaining home for her mother. Sarah was a grown woman, after all. She appeared strong and she had her husband and her parents—even her sister to support her. Did she really need Martha as well? Those thoughts fought with his kinder side, when he was grateful for Martha's devotion towards her family and admired her for her loyalty.

Since it was still early evening, he hadn't undressed yet, so he tucked his phone in his pocket and went downstairs. Before heading to the workshop, he looked in the refrigerator for something to eat. Hazel had brought over a meatloaf for them earlier, but he was embarrassed to take any back with him, even though Hazel had suggested it.

Maybe he'd find some left in the small refrigerator they kept running at the shop. He threw a light jacket over his shirt and covered his head with his straw hat before walking next door to the shop. Sure enough, there was a nice hunk of meatloaf left. He cut it in half and ate it cold, adding a slice of wheat bread from the countertop. As he finished up, he heard a faint knock on the back door, and when he opened it, Hazel stood before him, face reddened from tears.

"Oh, it's you," she said, disappointment in her voice. "I saw the light on and figured it was Jeremiah."

"Just me. It's getting dark already, Hazel. Come on in. Jeremiah left over an hour ago, when I did. What's going on?"

"Why are you here then?" she asked, remaining by the door.

"I knew I wasn't ready for sleep, so I figured I'd get some work done. Is anything wrong?"

"Everything," she sputtered as she covered her face with her hands and began weeping loudly. "Jeremiah broke off with me. He says I don't love him enough. He was real mad at me, Paul."

"Why would he think that? Listen, come in and sit down. You can talk to me. I know things will work out with you two."

He led her over to two side chairs in the private area of the shop and she sat and tried to stop crying. He reached over and patted her shoulder, wishing he'd remained home.

"Oh, Paul, you're so kind. Maybe he's right. Maybe I've never gotten over you."

Uh, oh. "That's not true, Hazel. He just doesn't understand women."

"Oh," she said smiling through her tears. "And you do?"

"Well, better than he does. I think." This felt like dangerous territory.

"I'm afraid I am still in love with you, but I understand you don't like me anymore."

"It's not that I don't like you, Hazel, you know that. It's just…"

"I know. You and Martha. I just thought maybe now that you've postponed your wedding, maybe you and she were having doubts. Forgive me. I even prayed that was happening." She let out a new torrent of tears. "That was so wrong of me. I hope *Gott* forgives me."

Paul pushed his chair further away from hers. She looked about ready to pounce on him. This was scary stuff.

"You're safe," she managed to say through the tears. "For heaven sake, Paul, I'm not going to attack you."

Embarrassed, he tried to laugh, but it came out as a phony guffaw. He cleared his throat and spoke firmly. "Martha and I are still planning to marry, Hazel. I don't want to hurt you, but we've just put it off until her *mamm* gets through this cancer."

"And if she doesn't make it? Will Martha remain home to take care of her *daed*? What kind of love is that, Paul? You'd always come first in my life, for sure."

"Now, that's not nice to say about Martha. She's very devoted and that's a *gut* thing."

"Jah?"

"Jah." He said it with more conviction than he felt.

"I wish I'd never said anything to you about my feelings. Please don't tell Jeremiah what I said. I want it to work for us. I really do. He's a nice man. I think once we marry, I'll be able to forget about you."

"Hazel, you have to forget now. It wouldn't be fair to Jeremiah to marry him feeling the way you do."

"I guess you're right. How do I do that? How do

I turn off my feelings? I may have to move away so I don't see you anymore. I cook for *you*, Paul. If you weren't here, I'd let Jeremiah fend for himself. I know that sounds horrible."

Paul reached across the chasm, which had narrowed as she moved her chair closer to his, and prepared to pat her hand. Thinking better of it, he rose and leaned against a workbench and pulled on his suspenders. "You're a mighty *gut* cook, too, I'll say that," he added.

She stood up and Paul hoped she'd decided to leave, but instead, she came right over to him and put her arms around his waist and laid her head against his chest. Goodness! What was a man to do?

"Hazel, please. Don't do this."

"We used to love each other. Don't deny it, Paul. I don't know what happened, but I think we could love again."

He looked down at her lovely soft eyes and remembered how much he had cared about her once. He was lonely. She was distraught. His heart beat rapidly. He suddenly realized her lips were pressing against his. It was so wrong, yet it felt so right—at that vulnerable moment. Then, realizing what was happening, he pulled away and walked over to the window and looked out at the dark scene in front of him. What could he say to discourage her?

The moon was out in full, casting long shadows on the fresh spring grasses. Then he felt her beside him once again, and when he turned, he saw she'd removed her bonnet and was unpinning her long blonde tresses. Her lips invited him once more and he found himself wrapping his arms around her as he responded to her kiss. His hand stroked her lovely long hair. Then he withdrew and moved back. "Oh, Hazel, what are you doing to me? Please don't."

"I love you, Paul, more than anyone in the world. I'd always be faithful to you and care for you above all others. Give me a chance again."

He studied her lovely face, framed with her golden hair. Why had he left her? They had been close. Was this the answer for him?

"It's not fair to Martha or Jeremiah, Hazel. Please leave before we go any further. Let me think. I need to be alone."

"*Jah.* I understand." She stood back and quickly wrapped her hair into a bun and shoved a few hairpins in before covering it with her bonnet. "I'll leave now, Paul. I'm done with Jeremiah though. You're right. It wouldn't be fair of me to continue leading him on. I'll wait for you—no matter how long it takes." She turned and left.

Paul remained standing by the window, as he watched her ignite the lamps on the buggy and head slowly down the lane to the road.

His phone went off. He looked. It was probably Martha. He let it ring and then went over to the shelf and began the monotonous job of sanding. There'd be no sleep tonight.

Chapter Six

Martha drove the buggy back from the community phone, disappointed that Paul hadn't answered. It was only eight o'clock. Surely, he wouldn't be in bed quite yet. Maybe he was using a noisy tool. That was it. He most likely didn't hear the phone ring. When she got back, her parents were playing checkers on a card table they left set up in the sitting room. Sarah looked up and smiled at her daughter.

"What time does *Mammi* want to go to the phone shed tomorrow?" Sarah asked.

"I told her I'd check at nine in the morning. We have to be back in time to take you to your appointment."

"If you're not back in time, *Daed* will go with me. We can take the open buggy."

"But I want to be there for you."

"*Jah*, I know. That's very sweet of you, Martha. I sure appreciate everything you do for me."

"I just took three of your pieces, Sarah," her father said, a sparkle in his eyes.

"*Jah*, take advantage of a woman when she's talking."

"That's the only time I can win," he said chuckling. "Want to play the loser, Martha?"

"Sure, though I thought I'd write to Deborah tonight."

"*Jah*, that's more important," Sarah said. "And since your *Daed*'s gonna lose, you can play him tomorrow."

"Oh, just watch," he said as he took his next turn and removed another checker from the board.

"I think you're cheating," Sarah said, smiling over.

As Martha went upstairs, she heard their little exchange continue. They had such fun together. Hopefully, she and Paul would have a similar relationship. She wondered if she should tell him about her mother's suggestion they marry sooner; but no, he'd really push for the wedding if he knew that, and she still believed she should wait to know her mother's outcome before thinking of herself. Chemo would be started soon, which she knew her mother dreaded. Perhaps, since many years had passed from her last bout with cancer, they had better medication to treat the nausea and vomiting. She sure hoped so.

Martha wrote a four-page letter to her friend, Deborah. She asked her how she was dealing with her latest pregnancy and also about the children. Since Martha no longer went for the baptismal classes, she didn't see Deborah and her family as frequently. She also asked if they saw Paul as much now that he had his own business and had moved into the house on the property.

This time when Deborah had her baby, her family would have to step in to help. Martha would still be tied up with her mother.

Maybe she'd stop by Bishop Josiah's place when things slowed down. She didn't see any harm in talking to him about baptism. It would be good to get herself baptized, even if she didn't want to proceed with the wedding yet. After all, she never planned to leave the Amish, regardless of what lay ahead.

When she came back down the stairs, Daniel was sitting with her parents. Funny, she hadn't even heard the buggy.

"Hi, Daniel. I didn't hear you come in."

"I left the buggy by the road. I noticed the horse was limping a little tonight, so I didn't want him injuring himself more. I'll stop over at the vet's on my way back. I was just talking to your parents. I told your *mamm*, she looks real *gut*, considering."

"Well," Sarah said, smiling over. "You have to keep your spirits up for everyone's sake, for sure."

"*Jah*, I know you have a pretty worried *dochder*."

Sarah glanced over at Martha, who had the distinct impression that her mother was going to mention the marriage might proceed as originally planned. For some reason, she hoped it would not be mentioned.

"Want some *kaffi*?" Martha asked, turning her attention to Daniel.

"Sure. I have plenty of time. I could take you for a buggy ride, if you want."

"It's too dark out," she said quickly. "Do you need me to do anything first, *Mamm*?"

"*Nee*, you two sit and have a nice time together. Just like the old days, *jah*?" her grin looked mischievous, and Martha was not happy.

They decided to play gin rummy, and Daniel sat at the kitchen table while Martha went to get the cards from the desk in the sitting room. She avoided looking over at her parents, slightly annoyed at the encouragement her mother seemed to give Daniel anytime he showed up.

While he sat and shuffled the cards, Martha checked the coffee and then set two mugs on the table. "Do you want cookies, too?"

"I'd better not. I'm all sugared out. Molly keeps me supplied with her famous brownies and they're hard to resist."

Martha nodded, sat down and waited while he dealt the cards. They played for over an hour and then sat and talked about everything from the weather to the latest news with their mutual friends.

"So, you're back with Molly," Martha said once they ran out of subject matter. "I thought you were going out with an English *maed*."

"They're too different for me long term. Fun for a while, but I want to settle down and raise a family. You know that."

"Well, you seemed to be leading a pretty wild life for a while."

"*Jah*, and it had its fun moments, but it's time to be serious." He laid the cards aside and finished his coffee. "Want any more?"

"Nee. I guess I'll get back to my place. It was a busy day. I'm beat."

"*Danki* for checking with my *mudder*, Daniel. It's very considerate of you."

"She's a nice lady, Martha. I've always liked your family. Sometimes I enjoy being with you all more than with my own family. Of course, it doesn't mean I don't love them…"

"No, of course not. We've talked before about this. I know your family tends to be more serious."

He laughed aloud. "*Jah*, that's putting it mildly. I haven't seen my father smile in years. Don't know if he can, at this point."

"You seem to be lighter now. More normal."

He grinned over. "You taught me a lot. I'll be grateful forever for the time we were together. I know it was my fault it didn't work out, and I'm sorry, Martha. I hope you can forgive me. Especially for acting the way I did with you that day when…"

"It's forgotten. Of course, I forgive. Do I have a choice?"

"But you mean it, *jah*?"

"I do."

He rose from his chair and reached for his hat. Then he walked back to the sitting room to say good-bye to her parents. As he reached for the back-door handle, he made no attempt to touch Martha. He was living up to his end of their bargain. Good for him, she thought. They could be just friends, that was for sure.

Hopefully, Paul felt the same for Hazel, since she probably made herself present most evenings in order to spend time with Jeremiah. It would be a relief to have those two marry. One less thing to think about.

Before leaving, Daniel mentioned he was looking for homes for four kittens born six weeks before. "Do you want a couple more barn cats?" he asked Martha.

"I'll have to check with *Daed*, but it's hard to turn down cats. What color are they?" she asked.

"Two are striped and there's a yellow one and a white one with yellow markings."

"They sound adorable."

"If you want, I can come by and take you over to my

barn. Then you can pick out the ones you like. Probably just two though, Martha. I know you. You'll want them all."

"Okay. I'll check with *Daed* first, to make sure it's okay."

"How about tomorrow late afternoon sometime?" he asked.

"I guess that would work. We usually get home by three."

"Then I'll come around three-thirty. It shouldn't take long. I'm going to a baseball game with Molly at five."

Martha was alarmed to feel jealousy at his last remark. Goodness that was strange. "We can do it another day," she said.

"You'd better get your pick before Molly sees them. She told me she loves cats."

"Okay. Tomorrow it is. You don't have to come for me. I'll go over on my own."

"It's not a problem, Martha. I like to check up on your *mudder* as well."

It was settled. He'd pick her up. After he left, Martha joined her parents and mentioned his last remark about wanting to check the next day on her mother.

"Now ain't that sweet?" Sarah said, grinning from ear-to-ear.

"*Jah*, sweet," Martha said, trying not to grimace.

Her father agreed about adopting two more cats for the barn, but he didn't express any thoughts on Daniel's deep concern for his wife's health. He'd never cottoned up to Daniel—not since the fight, and he had reservations about the young man's motives for coming so frequently.

* * *

The next day, after breakfast, Martha took her grandmother to the phone shed so she could make an appointment for her *dawdi*. When she got off the phone and climbed back in the buggy, Martha considered calling Paul at work, but decided against it. The sky was overcast and there was a prediction of heavy rain. It would be better to get home.

The appointment was set up for the following week, and Martha wrote it down on the calendar when they got back. Between radiation appointments, doctor visits and market days, the calendar was nearly full. How on earth would her parents be able to attend to all these things without her? After all, her father was still a farmer and even though Lizzy's sons came and helped him with the fields, there was still much for him to do every day.

Chapter Seven

Rose spent over an hour editing chapters for her next book as she waited for the weather to warm up before starting her day's adventure. With the suggestion of her hostess, Phyllis Forbes, she planned to check out some of the small towns outside of Lancaster, since they figured the Troyers would most likely have a farmhouse in the countryside. Today she planned to stop for lunch in Strasburg and then talk to some of the merchants. Mailboxes might offer a clue as well, though she'd already noticed most of the names were Lapp, Zook, and Miller, many of whom were directly related to each other.

After a large country breakfast of fried eggs with local bacon and homemade bread, she made her way south-east from Lancaster. If she saw a settlement with the right kind of shop, she'd stop and question the owner about the Troyer family. It turned out the name was fairly common here, but so far no one knew of a Melvin or Sarah. If there was a younger person in the shop, she'd actually ask about a Martha Troyer, as well. Nothing seemed to be a strong lead, so she stopped for lunch around two, after the crowds had been served.

Her waitress was actually an Amish woman, and she made every attempt to be helpful. She suggested looking in the Paradise Township area, specifically mentioning the town of Ronks. Rose did not give specific reasons for her search, but just explained she'd been raised Amish in Ohio and wanted to find some relatives in Pennsylvania, if possible.

Her resistance was unexpectedly low when it came to purchasing some of the Amish treats she remembered, and she bought a couple of sticky buns and whoopee pies from a local bakery to satisfy her craving.

She was even tempted to buy a *kapp*, but felt foolish trying it on with her short hair and English clothing.

By mid-afternoon, she'd stopped at half a dozen shops and spoken with at least ten people. She felt no closer to her objective, but at least she had eliminated a whole area. When she returned to her room, she removed her heels and laid on the bed, which was made with a handmade quilt in shades of pink. She fell asleep almost immediately and woke an hour later, somewhat confused about her surroundings. When she was fully awake, she wrote in her journal about her day. Would she ever find the young woman she'd given birth to? And had the young woman forgiven her for putting her up for adoption? Though she'd never intended to speak to her daughter, Rose now realized she would want to, if the opportunity arose. She felt a need to know if she'd been forgiven.

Promptly at half past three, Daniel pulled up at the Troyer farm in his open buggy. Martha had been watching for him, and she pulled on a shawl as she told her mother where she was headed. She noted the broad smile on her *mamm*'s face. She obviously still had hopes for Martha to change her mind and return to Daniel. Why then, did she seem to push Martha to marry this fall? She questioned her mother's sincerity.

When they got to the barn, the mother cat was grooming her babies and she looked none too happy when Martha knelt down and picked up the smallest kitten, placing it in her lap to pet. "This one is adorable, Daniel. Listen to his little purring motor." She giggled as she held her up to her cheek. Daniel grinned over.

"I think she likes you. How about her sister with the stripes?"

"*Jah*, she's a cutie, too. Poor *mudder*. She's not going to be happy if all her kittens disappear the same day."

"I'll make Molly wait a few days before I show them to her. Better not tell her I gave you first choice."

"I don't talk to Molly much. She has her own group of friends at church. I don't think she really likes me."

"Maybe she's jealous."

"Jealous of me? Why on earth would she be?"

"I think you know the answer to that." He looked at his watch. "I guess I'd better take you back now. So, you want the striped one, too?"

"*Jah*." She picked it up and held the two together. "*Danki*. I still feel bad about the *mudder* cat. She's staring at me."

"I'll pet her and you can sneak them out."

"Say hello to Molly for me."

"I'd rather be with you, you know."

"Daniel...you promised."

"I know. You're right. No more talk like that. I know I don't stand a chance, but at least we're *gut* friends."

"*Jah*, real *gut*," she said, nodding over as he held the

kittens while she climbed in. Then he handed them over and made his way to the driver's side. Martha held them carefully on her lap and concentrated on thinking up names for the new members of her family.

Two days passed before Paul called Martha's cell phone. Still no sign she'd activated it. He'd have to wait for her to call him. She apparently hadn't tried since the evening he'd found himself alone with Hazel. He hadn't been able to get her visit out of his mind and when he allowed himself to relive it, he was more confused than ever. Of course, he loved Martha. He'd always love her, but…

The next morning, Jeremiah was unusually quiet as he worked alongside Paul and Ben, and seemed to avoid looking in Paul's direction. Ben seemed oblivious to the silence between the two men. Paul considered bringing up the subject of Hazel, but decided it could lead to division in his relationship with Jeremiah, so nothing was said.

When suppertime arrived the second day without Hazel providing them with one of her delicious meals, Jeremiah looked over at Paul.

"She's not gonna be bringing any more meals, Paul. Sorry."

"It's okay." He studied the drawer he was working on and never looked up.

"Don't you wonder why?" Jeremiah asked moments later.

"It's not really my business," Paul said, regretting the tone he'd used. Surely, he cared about his friend and wouldn't want to intentionally hurt him further. He looked over. "But if you want to talk, please feel free."

Since Ben had left to run errands, now would be the time—if ever.

Jeremiah put his tools down and folded his arms after taking a seat on the other side of the room. "Please come sit a minute."

"Sure." Paul wiped his hands on his apron and went over to sit across from Jeremiah.

"We broke up."

"I'm sorry."

"Don't you wanna know why?"

"If you want to tell me, sure."

Jeremiah cleared his throat before proceeding. "I think she still cares about you."

"She knows about Martha."

"It doesn't seem to matter. She admitted she doesn't love me—not enough to be my wife."

"Honest, Jeremiah, I haven't done anything to encourage her feelings."

"I believe you. But I guess she's just smitten and that's all there is to it. I can't marry a girl who loves another."

"Of course not. I know it hurts, but one day, you'll meet another *maed*, for sure."

"I'm just real disappointed. I'd even taken her home to meet the family."

"Maybe she'll change her mind," Paul said. "Good grief! Martha and I hope to marry. She knows that."

"Well, it hasn't happened yet, and I guess Hazel takes that as an encouraging sign. Do you think you could talk to her and make it clear about your feelings?"

"*Jah*. Actually, I did."

"When?" Jeremiah's mouth dropped open.

"I guess it was the night you broke up. She came here looking for you and I was working extra time."

"Why didn't you tell me before?"

"I didn't see the point."

"So, what did you say?"

"I told her I planned to marry Martha. What else could I say?"

"Hmm. Did she cry?"

"Jah."

"I'm surprised she would talk about it. Wasn't she embarrassed?"

"Maybe a little."

"Well, at least you tried. *Danki*. She's fighting a losing battle."

"Jah, she sure is."

"So, when are you and Martha gonna actually go through with it? Do you have to wait another year?"

"Probably. It's all because of her *mudder* and the cancer. Martha's very devoted to her. Maybe even more than most *dochders*, since she was adopted."

"I guess so. It's got to be hard on you both, since you don't see much of each other. At least she has that cell phone you bought for her."

"She won't use it."

"Why not? Goodness, she's a grown woman. She should be able to do as she pleases."

"She doesn't want to upset her parents."

"But she's upsetting you, right?"

"I understand her reasons. I try to, anyway."

"Will she really move away when you get married? I mean, she's so close to her family, and since she's their only child and all…"

"She said she would. I really need to get to see her

in person—soon. I may take tomorrow off, since we're almost caught up on our orders."

"Sure, plus you've put in a lot of extra hours. Take a couple days. Are you going to surprise her again?"

"Probably not this time since I need to know if it's okay for me to show up there. Her *mudder* is getting radiation treatments, as you know. I don't want to get in the way."

"Mmm. I'm sure Martha wouldn't think of it that way. I bet she misses you as much as you miss her."

"I hope."

Paul's mood improved, just knowing he'd be seeing Martha again. Hopefully, Skip would be available to drive him. This thing with Hazel hadn't helped his mood—not one bit!

Chapter Eight

Martha waited impatiently for Paul to answer her call, after already waiting over fifteen minutes to use the community phone. She thought about the convenience of the cell phone sitting at home in her dresser drawer. Maybe she was too concerned about not using it.

On the fifth ring, Paul's voice answered. "Hi, Martha."

"How did you know it was me?" she asked, smiling into the phone.

"I guess because no one else ever calls me at this time of day. Why haven't you called sooner?"

"I tried a couple times, but you never answered."

"Well, it doesn't really matter. I have *gut* news! I'm taking off work tomorrow and I have my driver lined up to bring me out to see you."

"Wonderful-*gut*! I'm so glad. How long can you stay?"

"I guess it depends on things at your end. I was hoping to stay overnight, but if it wouldn't work out, I'd understand."

"I think it will be fine. I'll check with *Mamm* when I

get back home and if it doesn't work, I'll use the phone you gave me to let you know."

"You're using it now?"

"I haven't used it yet, but for an emergency, which this kinda would be, I think it would be okay. It's getting dark and I don't want to go out in the buggy again tonight."

"I'm glad it'll come in handy."

"*Jah, danki.* I forgot to thank you before."

"It's okay. I charged it up before giving it to you. I hope it still works. I thought I'd hear from you right away, though. How's your *mudder* doing?"

"She's doing as well as you can expect, considering. She never complains."

"*Jah*, she's a strong woman, for sure."

"I know she's concerned about her *daed*, though. He's been feeling poorly. He finally said he'd see his doctor. In fact, he has an appointment next week."

"Do you think it's his heart?"

"I don't know. He almost passed out a few days ago, and he drinks water all the time."

"He's getting old, I guess."

"Maybe that's it. Anyway, it will be *gut* to get his doctor to see him."

"Are you getting enough rest, Martha? You have to take care of yourself, you know."

"I sleep *gut*—most of the time. Oh, I'm so glad you're coming, Paul. It's real hard being so far apart."

"It doesn't have to be like this," he reminded her once again.

"Don't. You know how I feel."

"Sorry. I'll try not to mention it."

"I'd appreciate that."

Silence.

"Well, I have the driver scheduled for half past eight in the morning, so it won't be long now."

"Unless I have to cancel it, Paul. But I'm pretty sure it will be okay with everyone."

"You'll call me tonight, if it isn't? Right?"

"*Jah*. I'll ask as soon as I get home."

They said good-bye and she made her way back to the buggy, just as Daniel went by in his open buggy with a girl next to him. It was getting dark, but she could make out the features of her friend, Molly, who smiled and waved over. Perhaps they were going to a meeting together. She admitted to having a stab of jealousy—surely not because of Daniel dating someone. Most likely, it was because she wished Paul was there with her. A moment of loneliness pulled at her heart. *Jah*, that was it, for sure. She had no interest whatsoever in Daniel. That was history. And tomorrow, she'd be with her future husband. That's what she'd concentrate on. A smile crossed her face as she encouraged her horse, Chessy, to make his way home a little quicker.

There was no need to call and cancel Paul. Her parents seemed pleased he was coming.

Martha baked up some lemon bars and wrapped up a few for her grandmother. She also had several oatmeal cookies left from a batch she'd made a few days before, and included them in the *toot* for her grandfather. Then she walked over to the *dawdi haus* to tell her grandparents about Paul's visit.

After sitting with them for a few minutes, she rose to leave.

"Now bring him around when he's here," her *mammi*

said, as she followed her to the door. "We want to get to know the young man better, if you're gonna marry him some day."

"I will, *Mammi*, but we won't have much time together, so we won't stay long."

"Ah, young love. I understand, *liebschdi*. I was young once myself." Martha leaned over and kissed her grandmother's cheek before she turned to open the door.

That night, Martha had trouble sleeping. Her mind raced. Sometimes she'd have a fleeting dream about Paul, but other times it was Daniel sneaking in on her subconscious. There were times she forced herself to put Daniel's face out of her mind. Why it was troubling her at this point, she had no idea. She certainly didn't doubt her abiding love for Paul.

At ten-thirty, she heard the car pull into the drive and she made her way out to greet Paul, wiping her hands on her apron first. Her father heard the car as well, and stopped grooming his horses to join her by the car. Paul shook her father's hand and then nodded over at Martha, a grin sweeping his face, making his eyes dance. Her heart leaped and she wished they could be alone in order to embrace.

After a few pleasantries were exchanged and the driver, Skip, made arrangements for the pick-up the following day, Paul followed Martha into the house and greeted her mother. Then Martha offered him a lemon bar with some fresh coffee, and they sat together alone in the kitchen. After a quick kiss, they sat holding hands, while drinking coffee with their free ones. It was wonderful to be together again, and any doubts Martha had brewing about their future, dissipated into thin air.

After about an hour, they went over and sat with her grandparents for a while, and then went walking along the property line in the back until they came to a sheltered area with several budding trees, which offered filtered shade from the sun.

Paul embraced her and touched her lips with his. Hazel's sweet face suddenly appeared in his mind, causing shame and guilt, which forced him to pull away.

"What's wrong?" Martha asked, concern showing in her eyes.

"I'm sorry. I don't know," he said hesitantly. "Let's walk some more."

They walked slowly now and he sighed audibly as they came to a fence and stopped. Three of the neighbor's horses came over to greet them, but Martha stood back and folded her arms. "Something's not right, Paul. You're acting really weird. You'd better explain."

"It's nothing. Really."

She continued to stand still and without uttering a word, waited for a response.

"Oh, Martha. I guess I'm just lonely. I want us to be together."

"We talk about this every time we're together. Why can't you be more patient? If you really loved me, you'd be more understanding. It's not forever."

"I know. I know, but sometimes it feels like forever. I'm a man, Martha. I have needs."

"Well, join the human race. We all have feelings, but you have to control those feelings. We're not animals."

"You really don't understand, do you? I need a wife!"

"Well, if you truly loved me, you'd be willing to wait without constantly complaining. Don't you think I'd like to be married?"

"I'm not really sure anymore. You treat your mother like she's the child. I'm sure she could handle this without being coddled by her daughter."

"Coddled? Really? That's what you think I'm doing? What if it was your mother and—"

"My mother wouldn't expect me to babysit her! She'd encourage me to move out and lead my own life!"

"Well, my mother said the same thing! She told me to get married this fall! She's not selfish!"

"Wait!" Paul stood back and gaped at her. "You mean she's even told you to marry me, and you still won't? What's that all about?"

"I know I'm needed here. She's just being kind. I know she really wants me to stay."

"Or is it that you aren't real sure about your feelings anymore?"

"Don't be ridiculous!"

"Am I? Okay, I may as well tell you. Hazel came to me the other night. She still loves me and wants me back!"

"Is that so! Well, Daniel would be thrilled if I left you for him!"

They stood facing each other, suddenly aware of the words between them. The scalding, unretractable words that sliced into their very hearts. After several painful minutes, Paul reached over for Martha's hands. She withdrew them from his reach and turned. Then without another word, she ran back to the house, never looking back.

Paul stood motionless. What had he done? Why had those words even entered his mind? His dreams seemed shattered. Had he destroyed any chance of having this lovely woman for his bride? Worse than that—did he really care?

* * *

Martha reached the house, ran through the back door, past her mother and up to her room. She threw herself on her bed, but no tears came—just a pounding of her heart against the mattress. She could feel the beating in her head. That's all she could feel. No emotion, just a dead feeling. As if a dream had burst and all that was left were shards of broken glass. Was it her heart?

An hour passed. No one had come up to see her. No one. Then she heard a car on the gravel and she sat on the edge of the bed where she could look out. It was Paul's driver. Paul was opening the passenger side of the front. She couldn't see his face, but his demeanor was one of defeat. He never looked back, but threw an overnight bag across the top of the seat and then sat and closed the door behind him. A few moments later, he was gone. Gone from her life. She stared at the empty drive and shivered.

It would soon be time to take her mother for her radiation. In robotic motion, she tidied up her strands of loose hair and slipped her shoes on before going out to ready the buggy. Life goes on.

Chapter Nine

The following week, there was no communication between the two young lovers. Several times, Paul started to initiate a call, but then placed his phone back in his pocket. He and Jeremiah spoke only when they had to, and it was always about business. Ben was quieter than usual, but kept to his work. There was no sign of Hazel.

Then on Friday evening, Paul made a visit to his friends, Deborah and Ebenezer Lapp. It had been a couple of weeks since he'd stopped by, and he missed seeing their children. He used to feel needed when Ebenezer failed to contribute to the raising of their boy triplets and girl twins, but Eb had made a turnaround and helped his wife with the many chores she faced.

Paul figured Hazel and her sister Wanda still helped Deborah as much as possible. The three sisters were very close. By this time, Paul thought Hazel would be back at her home with her parents, but when he pulled up, he noted her buggy was secured at the hitching post. Her horse was not in sight and was most likely grazing with the other horses.

He could have walked in without knocking, which he

often had done in the past, but tonight he knocked and waited to be invited in. Hazel appeared at the door and he noted her expression, a mixture of shock and delight.

"Come in, Paul. Deborah was just asking if I'd seen you lately."

"Who is it?" Eb's voice came from the front room.

"Your friend, Paul. Speaking of the devil," she added and then covered her mouth with her hand. "Oh, I'm so sorry, Paul. You know I didn't mean it."

Paul laughed. "I hope not. It's a strange expression, *jah*?"

They walked together to the front room where the three boys were playing with blocks. When they saw Paul, they jumped up and surrounded him with their arms, nearly knocking him over. Everyone laughed at their wild enthusiasm. Deborah came down when she heard all the excitement. The twins had just been put to bed for the night.

Paul nodded over.

"Hi, stranger," she said. "We've missed seeing you. Too busy making a fortune to check on your friends?"

"It has been real busy, but we have a third carpenter now and we're finally seeing daylight, so I'll probably be here more often."

"Sit. I shouldn't tease you. How about some fresh apple pie? Hazel made three pies for us this morning."

"I can't say no to her pies," he said, looking over at Hazel, who was trying to hide a blush.

"Boys, settle down, and let *Onkel* Paul catch his breath. Maybe you'd better eat it in the kitchen, Paul. Otherwise you might end up with only one bite, the way the boys love to eat her pies."

"I'll cut you a piece," Hazel said, as she led the way to the back.

"I'll join you in a few minutes," Eb said. "We have to get these *bu* to bed first."

"Take your time," Paul called back. He took a seat and watched as Hazel reached for a pie server and a fresh plate. Her *kapp* was askew and a few strands of hair had escaped altogether and rested on her shoulder. It brought back memories of the evening she removed her *kapp* and released her hair for him. He had been very tempted to do something he'd be ashamed of after. She was a beautiful woman, and he was a young man with passion. Not an easy situation. Being a strong Amishman did not make him immune from temptation. Even now, it was awkward to be alone with her.

She set the plate in front of him and brushed against his chair. "Want a glass of milk with it?" she asked.

"*Jah*, please." He picked up his fork and concentrated on the dessert. After the first bite, he complimented her.

"*Jah*, I've been blessed with the gift of cooking, I've been told," she said. "It should come in handy someday, I guess."

Paul ate the rest of the pie in silence while Hazel busied herself with wiping off the counters, though they looked shiny before she even attempted it. Paul realized she was uncomfortable as well.

"Have you and Jeremiah made up yet?" he finally asked, as he set his fork on the empty plate.

"I haven't seen him since you and I…since we talked last time. I guess it's over."

"And you're okay with that?"

"I have no choice in the matter."

"If you did, would you try to make up?"

"Paul, why are you asking me these questions? I know it's over as far as you and I are concerned. I've finally accepted that fact. Don't make it harder on me by giving me false hope. Please."

"Hazel, I'm sorry." He looked down at the table as he folded his paper napkin into a small square.

"Have you set a date yet for your wedding?" she asked as she sat down across from him.

"Nee."

"Still waiting for her *mudder* to get better?"

"You could say that." He stopped handling the napkin and pushed his chair back slightly and folded his arms. "Things aren't great between us right now."

"I'm sorry."

"Are you? Really?"

She looked directly into his azure blue eyes. "Okay, I'm not sorry. Not one bit, but what does it mean really?"

"Maybe nothing, but I've been reflecting on things. Mainly the way I treated you."

"Paul, you were always honest with me. I appreciate that. Though I was heartbroken when you told me you didn't love me, I respected you for your honesty. I think you're a wonderful-*gut* person. The other thing is, I don't want to be hurt again. I couldn't take it. I'd rather be single than feel that kind of pain again. So, unless it's really over between you and Martha, with no chance of it changing, I'm not going to get involved in any way with you."

"I understand. I'm not really asking you to. I have real mixed feelings right now. I don't know what's going on inside me, to tell you the truth. Can a man be in love with two girls at the same time?"

"Love?" her light brows came together slightly. "You think you might love Martha *and* me? Seriously?"

"I don't know. I'm just thinking out loud, I guess. The other night…after you left… I couldn't get you out of my mind."

"Don't." She covered her face. "I don't want to hear this."

"I'm sorry, Hazel. I'm not being fair—either to you or Martha. Maybe I'll just move away and start all over."

"Don't talk like you're *ab im kopp*."

"Maybe I am crazy. I've never been so confused. I may as well tell you. I went to see Martha and we were arguing about putting off the wedding and she told me her *mamm* had actually suggested we get married in the fall. She was encouraging it."

"But Martha didn't want to?"

"Apparently not. She treats her *mudder* like she's a child. I can't take it anymore."

"I don't understand her, Paul. I love my *mudder* with all my heart, but I wouldn't put off my marriage—not when there are so many others to watch over her and be there for her. That is a strange love."

"I also told her I saw you."

"I'm sure that made her happy."

"She sees that guy, Daniel, so we're kind of even."

"Maybe they're just friends."

"Like us, Hazel? Is that what we are? Just friends?" His voice had lowered almost to a whisper.

"You're doing it again, Paul. Breaking my heart."

"I'm so sorry. Forgive me." He rose from his seat and knelt beside her, reaching for her hands.

"I want you to kiss me, but don't. Please don't." Her voice was barely audible.

"*Onkel* Paul," a voice from the hall called out. "Read us a story, please." It was Luke, one of the triplets, and he suddenly appeared by their side.

"I'll be up in a minute, Luke. Go tell the others."

The boy ran out of the room to obey Paul's request. Hazel stood up and Paul moved a couple feet away.

"I need to get home, Paul. I'll pray for you. And for Martha. And even for myself. I don't know how this is all going to end, but we can't live like this. None of us can."

"I'll stay in touch."

"That's up to you." She walked down the hall to say good night to the others. Paul walked slowly behind her. As he climbed the stairs to read to the boys, she looked up. There was no smile. Her eyes glistened from unshed tears forming.

Was he destroying the people he cared about most in the world? Gott *help me*, he said silently as he went in to read to the children.

Chapter Ten

For the last week, Rose had spent hours each day trying to locate her daughter or the family. She'd spoken with dozens of people, hoping to get a clue as to their whereabouts. So far, nothing had come of it and she decided she'd go back home to Ohio the day after the scheduled book signing. There was little hope of realizing her dream.

Her agent called and asked if she would prepare a short talk to give before selling the books. There had been much interest in her upcoming signing and the manager of the bookstore had contacted the agent. Rose agreed and after breakfast, she went back to her room and made a few notes for her upcoming public talk. She'd keep it short. Maybe take a few questions. Sometimes that was easier than doing all the talking herself.

When she was done, she decided to head for Paradise, since she'd pretty much been to every other highly populated Amish area within a ten-mile radius of Lancaster. Even though her errand had not proved successful, she had enjoyed the lovely scenery and the friendly people she'd encountered during her stay. She and the innkeeper, Phyllis, agreed to keep in touch. It had stirred up a multitude of memories, most good, some—not so much, but she felt kindlier in her mind towards her family and decided to try to get in touch with a couple of her sisters when she returned home. She hoped her mother was still living. If she was, she would try to communicate with her as well as her siblings. Enough years had passed. She figured she'd been forgiven for leaving by now.

As she sat at a counter that afternoon in Paradise, treating herself to an ice cream sundae, she mentioned her search for the Troyer family to the young waitress, who served her.

"Oh, I don't know any Sarah or Melvin," the girl behind the counter said as she wiped down the stainless ice cream containers. "But I know a girl named Martha. She's about my age, I guess."

Rose dropped her spoon and the clanking as it landed on the tile floor, startled her. "Yes, Martha. That's who I really want to know about."

"We've met right here. She comes in for ice cream sometimes, usually with a good-looking guy. Dreamy blue eyes. We've talked a lot in the past. She's real nice. She even helped take orders one day when I got slammed." The girl replaced the spoon and then came around the counter to retrieve the dropped one.

Rose was sure her heart could be heard from the road. She tried to sound casual. "Oh, I'm sorry, I should have picked it up." Then she added, "Do you know where she lives?"

"Not really. Not too far, I guess. They come in a buggy." She turned towards a young man, who had just taken a seat four stools away. She excused herself and went to take his order.

So, Martha was still in the area. It sounded like she was single, though maybe spoken for. What was the next step? She couldn't exactly camp out at the ice cream parlor night and day, and maybe Martha only came once a month. Rose picked up the fresh spoon and took another mouthful of ice cream, though if she'd been asked, she wouldn't have been able to say what flavor she was eating.

When the girl finished making up an ice cream cone for the young man, he paid her and left the shop. The girl returned to Rose. "Do you live around here?"

"No, I'm from Ohio. Could I impose upon you, and leave a letter for you to give the girl, Martha, when she returns?"

"Sure. Why not? Is she a relative?"

"Uh, sort of. I'll sit over at the table by the window, if I may, and write the letter. I don't have an envelope—"

"I have a used one in my purse you can have. It had an ad in it, but I was going to heave it anyway."

"You're very kind."

Rose finished her sundae and moved over to the table where she found her notepad in her purse and wrote a short letter. It was not easy to know what to say.

Dear Martha,
You don't really know me, but I am the woman who gave birth to you twenty years ago. Not a day has passed that I haven't thought of you and wondered how you were doing. I'd made an agreement when your family adopted you to stay out of your life, which I have done—until now. I fig-

*ure you are old enough to handle it, if we should
ever have an opportunity to meet. It is my greatest
desire to see you in person. To get to know you,
at least a little. I hope you have forgiven me for
giving you to another to raise.*

*If you decide not to pursue this any further, I
will understand, but I am hoping—and praying—
that you will contact me. I live in Ohio, but I can
travel anytime, since I'm a writer and can take
my computer wherever I go. I write Amish books
under a different name and am actually doing a
book signing in Lancaster before I go back home.
I'll write my address and my phone number down,
just in case you should decide to try to reach me.*

*In sincere love,
Rose Esh*

She reread it, added the information, and then folded
it and tucked it into the envelope the clerk had given her.
She scratched out the writing on the front and wrote
her daughter's name on it. When she handed it over, the
young woman took tape and sealed it. "I'll keep it in
my personal drawer in the back, but I promise to give
it to her next time she comes in."

"Thank you so much. You have no idea what this
means to me."

"I can tell it's important. I hope things work out for
you."

That one meeting changed everything for Rose. It
had been worth all the effort to be this close to find-

ing her daughter. Maybe she'd never hear a word from her, but if God was behind all this, someday she would.

Nancy sat nervously next to her husband, Rubin, as they waited to be called into the doctor's office. Though she tried to be optimistic, she dreaded the diagnosis forthcoming. Sarah and Martha sat across from them and flipped through old magazines, with little comprehension of the words they read. Each of them was fearful of the outcome.

At last, the elderly couple was taken back to the small examining room. Due to the small space and the fact Rubin would be undressed, Sarah and Martha waited behind.

The nurse took his blood pressure, temperature, and checked his weight. Then she laid a wrap for him to wear and after she left, he complained about the enormous size. "They must think I weigh five hundred pounds."

"One size fits all," his wife said, attempting humor.

"I guess."

Several minutes later, there was a knock on the door and his general physician, Dr. Butler, came in and nodded as he took a seat by the computer. After typing in a few notes, he rolled the stool back and folded his arms. "So, what's going on, Rubin?"

"I'm doing okay, but my family's been nagging me to come in and complain."

The doctor looked over at Nancy with a half-smile. "Maybe you should tell me what's going on then."

"He's so weak, he has trouble doing anything. Last week, I thought he was going to pass out. I know there's something wrong, but he's the most stubborn Amishman I've ever met!" She wiped an eye and leaned back in her chair, her lips clamped tight.

"Are you experiencing any pain? Chest pain? Abdominal?"

"Once in a while. Not all the time," Rubin admitted.

"Well, let's take a listen to that heart of yours." The doctor came over to the examining table and used his stethoscope, both on his chest and his back. He repeated it. Not a word. Then he checked the nurse's notes about his blood pressure and other statistics.

"Things sound pretty good," he began, "but you've lost some weight. Let's get some blood work done. Do you get thirsty more than normal?"

"He's always drinking water, doctor, and then he has to go to the bathroom a hundred times every night. We don't sleep together anymore. I wasn't getting any rest."

He nodded and looked at Rubin. "We'll need a urine sample as well. I assume that won't be a problem."

Rubin chuckled. "That's far easier to give than my blood."

Dr. Butler smiled back. "I'll also ask you to fast for eight hours before coming back to the lab for additional blood work. You can do that tomorrow or the next day."

"What are you looking for?" Rubin asked.

"Any abnormalities, but it's possible you're diabetic or pre-diabetic. As far as your heart is concerned, your heartbeat is strong and regular. The procedure they did seems to be working for you. I'll examine you further now, before sending you to the lab. You can lie back and I'll check your abdomen."

Martha looked over at Sarah while they waited. "I'm nervous, *Mamm*. Are you?"

"Well sure. It's normal to be concerned, but my *daed*'s a strong man and I think he'll get through this. Whatever it is. I'm worried about you though, Martha. You ain't been right since Paul came and went so fast."

"It's okay. I just don't want to think or talk about him right now. I have enough on my mind."

"I fear you two are having real problems. I sure hope I'm not the reason."

"Oh, *Mamm*," Martha said as she laid her magazine aside. "No, not at all. I'm just unhappy with Paul right now. We'll make up, for sure. I actually wrote to him last night."

"That's *gut*. Did you mail it yet?"

"*Nee*. I may not. I don't know, I have to think about it some more first."

"Don't think too long. It's harder to make up, the longer you're apart. It's because he wants to have a wedding soon, ain't?"

Martha raised her brows. "Why do you think that?"

"I know the young man is anxious to start his family. I told you not to delay on account of me, Martha. Of course, I'm disappointed about you moving away—especially now, but you have to lead your own life."

"I can't leave you now. All these years, you've dedicated your life to me. You and *Daed* have been the best parents a girl could ask for, and I wasn't even your blood child. How can I move on and desert you when you're so sick?"

"My dear Martha. I love you so much." Sarah wiped her tears. "But we could plan for next fall then. I know it's a long way off, but then Paul would know you want to marry. He probably thinks you don't care that much.

He's most likely hurting, Martha. Maybe worse than you."

"I hadn't thought of it that way."

They looked up at the same time as Nancy and Rubin returned to the waiting room.

After the lab work was done, they rode home together. Martha was the driver. Nancy filled them in on what had transpired.

"At least his heart is *gut*," Sarah said. "That was my biggest worry."

"*Jah*, I'm glad of it," Rubin said. "I guess I was more concerned than I let on, but diabetes ain't nothing to be excited about."

"*Nee,*" Sarah said, "but they have all kinds of medicine for it. Noah Fisher even gives himself shots, but he does okay."

"I forgot about that. He still farms, too. Maybe I'll get my energy back."

"That would be wonderful-*gut*, *Dawdi*," Martha added.

It seemed to Martha that her family was struggling with all kinds of health issues and it would be selfish of her to think of herself. Maybe she'd hold on to that letter she'd written for Paul until she was calmer. Between his attitude and his mentioning Hazel being in his life again, she wasn't sure what she really felt.

When they pulled up to the drive, a buggy was headed from the barn. It was Daniel. Goodness, he certainly showed up at the oddest times.

When she pulled over to let him pass, he stopped instead. "Have a few minutes before I'm supposed to be at work. Just talked to your *daed*, out in the barn. I gave him a hand with the milking," he said to Martha. "Have any *kaffi* left from breakfast?"

"I'll put a fresh pot on for you," Sarah said, smiling over.

"Everything okay?" he asked as he noticed the family was together.

"I'll explain once I get my horse unhitched," Martha said.

"Let me turn around and I'll help you," Daniel said as he went past their buggy to make a U-turn.

"What a nice young man," Sarah noted. "Always ready to help."

"It ain't always been that way," her father reminded her.

"Well, he's a changed man. Only *Gott* could do that."

"*Jah*, or he could be faking it to get your *dochder*."

"*Dawdi!* You think a person can fake it that much?" Martha asked.

"You'd better believe it. Now, hurry it up. I have to get in the house quick-like," he said to his granddaughter.

After the family got out of the buggy, Daniel and Martha unhitched the harnessing from the horse and led him to the pasture. "I hope everything's okay," Daniel said, looking over at Martha for a response.

"I guess you didn't know, but my *dawdi* hasn't been doing real *gut* lately, and he kept refusing to see the doctor. We were all concerned about his heart, but the doctor said it sounded fine. So now they're checking him for other things."

"Wow. Your family is really getting hit with health problems all of a sudden. *Gut* thing you're here to help,

Martha. It's important for families to live close to each other, that's for sure."

She knew he was referring to her possible move after marriage. She felt bombarded sometimes from every direction to remain at home. She'd heard it so many times, she was now questioning her own decision to ever move away, just for her future husband's sake. She worried Paul would be unwilling to start up his business here, even though there was a demand for good carpenters. Seemed a wee bit selfish to Martha, when she thought about it. Even though there was a house involved, weren't relationships more important? Her children would suffer if they had to visit their grandparents and other relatives just a couple times a year. It didn't seem fair to them either. Paul would have to think beyond himself if this marriage thing was going to work!

Daniel had said something else, but she hadn't heard his words. Her latest thoughts were somewhat of a shock to her. "Sorry, Daniel, you were saying?"

"Just that it's a beautiful spring day."

"Oh, *jah*. The lilacs are nearly in full bloom already. May is my favorite month."

"Mine, too! We have so much in common."

"We do?"

"*Jah*, we're both Amish, love *gut* food, not bad to look at, have nice families, and even like the same flowers."

Martha giggled. "What other flowers do you like?"

"Well," he said, hesitantly, "all of them really. Red roses are nice and tulips are pretty."

"Oh, I have to agree. What about cleome?"

"What are they?"

She laughed and shook her head. "They're not out yet, but when they are, I'll show you."

"You're staying home then, at least for another year?"

"It looks that way."

"I'm real glad, Martha. I'd miss you something terrible if I couldn't see you."

"I thought you were seeing Molly now."

"If she needs a ride, I help out. Don't forget, she lives only two farms away, but there ain't any real feeling there."

"On your part, or hers?"

"You sound curious. Does it matter to you?"

"Probably not," she said, looking down at the damp grass, as she headed towards the house, with Daniel next to her. She felt his hand as he reached for hers.

"No, Daniel. Nothing like that. We're friends. Nothing more. You promised."

"Sorry, I forgot myself. It must be the beautiful weather. I'm just happy, I guess."

She smiled over. "It's okay. I'm not mad, but I'm not ready for anything other than your friendship."

"I will behave then. Promise. So, when's that Paul guy coming to see you again? He was here last week, right?"

"Briefly. I'm not sure when—or if—he'll be coming for a while."

"That sounds like trouble brewing. Are you getting tired of his selfishness?"

"What do you mean?" She stopped and he did the same. They faced each other.

"Okay, this is how I feel, Martha. If he really loved you the way a man should, and wants to marry you, he would put everything aside for you. He would make sure you lived near your family, especially now with all this illness involved."

"But his business…"

"What's more important? Making money, or making your wife happy?"

"I guess when you put it that way…"

She began walking again, more slowly this time. "Why don't we walk a little more, but I don't want to talk about Paul anymore. We'll give *Mamm* a chance to get the *kaffi* made."

"Sounds *gut*, Martha. I love walking with you. You look so nice today. Is that a new *frack*?"

She smiled over. "As a matter of fact, it is. I finished sewing it last night. I love the color."

"The yellow goes *gut* with your dark eyes. You have really long eyelashes."

"I guess so."

"How long is your hair?"

"To my waist. Why?"

"I don't know. Just curious."

"Why are guys always talking about a girl's hair? I'd be vain to brag about it now, wouldn't I?"

"I'm sorry Amish people don't let the girls wear their hair down. That's one thing I like about the English."

"Did you ever go out with an English girl with real long hair?"

"*Jah*, one girl a few months ago. It was real pretty red hair."

"Did you love her?"

"No," he said, grinning. "I've only loved one girl my whole life."

"Molly?"

"You know better, Martha. Don't tease me. I'll always love you, no matter what."

She turned away from his gaze. At that moment, she feared his next move, as well as her response. She realized how lonely she was, and it frightened her.

Chapter Eleven

The unmailed letter sat in Martha's drawer for another week. She hadn't received a word from Paul. Her phone no longer was charged and she considered returning it to Paul, but was afraid it would end any possibility of them getting together again. She tried not to think about him, but it was difficult. Though sure she still loved him, there were times when she wondered if it was enough.

Daniel came by two more times during the week, but they talked only briefly. Martha appreciated his apparent concern for the family.

Her grandfather's test results came back and when Martha's mother called for the results, she was told it was diabetes. An appointment was made for the following week. When Sarah told the family, Martha was relieved it was not his heart. She knew very little about diabetes, but planned to go to the appointment, and perhaps sit in on the discussion. It would probably mean altering her grandfather's diet, which always included homemade desserts. He was not happy when that possibility was presented.

One morning, shortly after getting the test results,

Martha and Sarah sat in the *dawdi haus* with Martha's grandparents, as the coffee brewed to perfection.

"Would have been better if it had been my heart," her grandfather noted.

His wife clucked her tongue. "Don't be so silly, Rubin. I'll learn to cook with fake sugar, is all. You'll get used to it."

"I guess I don't have a choice now, do I?"

"Not even a teeny one," she said, as she waited by the stove for the coffee to finish brewing.

Aunt Liz knocked before entering the kitchen. Then she removed her shawl and draped it over a kitchen chair. After initial greetings and hugs were exchanged, she sat down next to her father. Martha went over to one of the cabinets and brought out another mug, setting it in front of her aunt.

"What, no goodies?" Liz asked.

"Not today," Sarah, remarked. "Not in front of *Daed*, anyway."

"I can look the other way," he said.

"Too much temptation."

Liz nodded. "You're right, *schwester*. So, you're going to change your way of eating, *Daed*."

"You're the tenth person to tell me that, Lizzy. I think I know by now. It's gonna be a nightmare."

Sarah and Lizzy looked over at their mother, who just shook her head. "He's worse than a *boppli*. My goodness, you'd think it was the end of the world."

"Kinda is," he said under his breath, as Nancy handed him a bright red Delicious apple on a plate.

"That's from last year, Nancy. Don't try to fool me."

"It's still hard. I've had it in the cellar. Now, stop making a fuss."

He bit into it. "Ain't too bad, I guess."

"Well, let's talk about something else, *Daed*, and get your mind off your problems," Lizzy said. Nancy came around with the coffeepot and filled everyone's mug and then took a seat.

Liz looked over at her niece. "Haven't talked to you lately, Martha. How are things going with you?"

"Okay."

"That sounds kinda weak. Has Paul been to see you lately?"

"He's pretty busy. I don't think he'll be here for a while."

"Mmm. I guess you have to make do with letters then, till you have more time."

"Maybe."

Liz looked from her niece's gloomy expression, over to her sister's. "Anyone want to tell me what's going on?"

"It's up to Martha," Sarah stated, looking over at her daughter.

"Not much to tell you. We kinda had an argument."

"Well, every couple runs into that once in a while. Try not to let it bother you too much. I'm sure he'll write, all full of apologies, real soon."

"It's been two weeks, almost," Martha said.

"Maybe you need to write first then," Liz suggested.

"I've written one, but didn't mail it yet."

"That's not going to help much," Lizzy said with a frown.

"He's being selfish, *Aenti* Liz," Martha began. "He keeps talking about getting married this fall, even though he knows I can't."

"Can't, or won't?" Liz asked.

Martha opened her mouth to answer, and then shrugged. "I'm not sure."

"I told her to go ahead and make plans," Sarah said, looking over at her sister. "She don't do it. It wonders me."

"I just don't think I should," Martha said. "You all need me now. I might be moving away, you know. It wouldn't seem right."

"We all want you to marry, but it sure would be nicer if the young man was from around here, I have to admit that," Sarah remarked.

"I think he'd probably move, if you asked him to," Liz said to Martha.

"I can't ask him. It would be selfish of me."

"Maybe he's just waiting for you to say the words. He'd do pretty *gut* here, I bet."

"I know, but he's in a partnership now and he's even working on a home where we'd live. It's right on the property he and his partner are buying. I don't think he'd want to give all that up."

"Maybe you have to put it out there, Martha. Just find out how important all that is to him." Liz wrapped her arms and waited for a response.

"That's not something I can do in a letter. We'd need to talk face-to-face."

"Then write and tell him you need to get together. You shouldn't keep trying to avoid the subject, Martha. In the end, a decision has to be made. Better to know now."

"I still love him."

"Of course. I'm sure you do, but love is fragile. Too much anxiety and anger can tear down the best relationships given enough time."

Sarah nodded at her sister's remarks. "That Daniel boy still comes around."

"Oh? I didn't think he was allowed here," Liz said.

"He's changed, Liz. He's so concerned for my health, dear *bu*."

"Oh, come now, sis. You think that's why he comes around? Because of you?"

"Well, it's one reason."

"He wants Martha, there's no question in my mind."

"He is different, though," Martha spoke up. "If we hadn't had that major fight, and I hadn't met Paul, things might have worked out for us."

"And then they could marry right away and settle right nearby," Sarah added. "Wouldn't that be just about perfect?"

"Except your *dochder* doesn't love the man," Liz stated, frowning.

"Oh, I'm so mixed up," Martha said, her eyes tearing up. "Sometimes I wish Paul and I had never met."

"I don't believe that. I saw the way you two were together. It sure looked like the love-bug had hit, and *gut* and hard."

"I'll write to him and tell him we need to see each other, and soon. You're right, *Aenti* Liz, I can't go on like this forever. I'm so confused. He has to prove I'm worth working for—even if it meant moving here and starting over."

Everyone nodded in agreement.

After supper that night, Martha excused herself early and went to her room to add to the original letter. She sat there a full hour, making several attempts, but finally, she gave up and went to brush her teeth and prepare for the night. It was harder all the time to fall asleep. She'd have to resolve her feelings soon, or she feared she'd be a basket case—or worse!

Rose stopped by the ice cream parlor on her way to the bookstore the day of the book signing. The girl she had talked to was busy, but she took the time to come over to tell her Martha had not been in as of yet. "I watch for her every day."

"Thank you so much. If you can make it to the bookstore before four, I'd be happy to give you a copy of my latest book."

"Maybe I can make it. I'm working till three. Thanks for the offer. It sounds like fun."

When Rose arrived at the bookstore, the manager, Loretta Knapp, had a desk all set up for her. Several dozen copies of her new book were arranged in piles on top. "We have more in the back, in case," the pleasant white-haired woman said. "Now I'll show you the area we have set up for your talk. We put up about thirty chairs, but if we need more, we can make room. There are already five or six people waiting. So, when do you go back to Ohio?" she asked Rose as they walked to the back of the shop.

"Tomorrow morning, I plan to take off early. I want to leave by six and beat the commuter traffic around Lancaster."

"Good idea. I'm so glad you were able to do this for us. We have a lot of Amish readers. Your books have always sold well for us."

"I'm glad." She glanced over at the people who had already arrived. They were all women, and most were over fifty. Others began to take seats, even a few men with their wives.

Once it was time to begin, Rose talked about her early life as an Amish girl, and after a few other remarks, she opened it up for discussion. After the usual, "When did you start writing?" "How do you get your ideas?" and "Do you still know any Amish?" she was asked about her reason for leaving the Amish religion. How much was she willing to tell?

"I had personal reasons for leaving. I'm sorry, I can't disclose them all, but it was a difficult decision."

"Are you sorry now?" another woman asked.

"Sometimes, though I believe it was the right decision at the time. Things were different then. People were less tolerant of young people when they got into trouble."

A few people looked at each other. They obviously guessed what her remarks were referring to. There were no further questions.

When it got quiet, Loretta stood and thanked everyone for coming and suggested that if they planned to purchase Rose's new book, they should line up for the signing.

Only two people left without buying her book. When the last person left with a signed copy, Rose glanced at the shop clock. They had asked her to stay until four, even though it was only three o'clock.

There were two customers wandering the aisles, who had not been there earlier. They nodded over as they perused the many choices of books.

Rose sat at the desk and caught up on her email by checking her cell phone. To use up time, she checked through her photos, eliminating some of her early ones, which no longer were significant enough to keep. Unexpectedly, the young woman from the ice cream shop appeared. She was slightly out of breath as she came directly over to Rose.

"Well, hi! I'm glad you made it," Rose said, reaching for the girl's hand, which she extended for a quick shake.

"How did you do? Many people come?"

"Not bad. I think we sold about forty books. The manager is going to let me know before they close. Well, this is it—my latest book," Rose said, lifting one up. "Would you like me to sign a copy for you?"

"Yeah, that would be cool."

Rose opened the book and reached for a pen. Then she looked up at the girl. "I'm sorry, I never asked you your name."

"Oh, it's Dawn. Dawn Hanson, but just write my first name." She stood watching as Rose added a biblical verse—Psalm 46:1.

"Golly, I don't have a Bible, but my grandma does."

"Oh, good. I just remembered, I have a small copy of the New Testament I keep in my purse. The book of Psalms is found in the Old Testament, but you might enjoy reading the New Testament, since it's all about Jesus." Rose reached into her purse and searched until she located the small red leather testament.

"Oh, I can pay you for it."

"No, please, it's a small token of my appreciation for helping me."

"I haven't done anything yet," the girl responded.

"But you will, if my daughter shows up." It was out before Rose even realized what she'd said.

"Martha is your daughter? Wow!" the girl said in awe. "That's exciting. And she doesn't know you yet?"

"No. Please sit with me. There's no one else around. I may as well tell you my story." Dawn sat across from Rose and leaned forward to catch every word. Rose explained what had happened as a young woman, even mentioning the father was an Italian student.

"It must have been hard to give her away."

"The hardest thing I've ever had to face. In those days, women—especially Amish women—were expected to save themselves for marriage."

"It's still a good idea, don't you think? I've never loved a guy enough to part with that…the virginity part."

"I'm glad. I hope you will stick to that plan. It would please God."

"I don't know much about God. My grandma goes to church and all, but my parents don't. They kinda make fun of her."

"I'm sorry to hear that. You should go with her some Sunday. I bet she'd be thrilled."

"Yeah, she mentions it a lot. Maybe I will. So, is your name really Astrid Flemming?"

"No, I use it for my pen name. It's Rose Esh. I was married, but I took up my maiden name again after my husband passed away."

"Oh, I'm sorry you're a widow."

"I'm used to being alone. It isn't so bad when you get used to it."

"I want to get married someday. I just haven't met the right guy yet, I guess," Dawn said, with a melancholy expression. She stood up and looked directly into Rose's eyes. "I really hope Martha comes in soon so I can give her the letter. Is it okay if I tell her I got to know you a little, and you're a real nice person?"

Rose laughed gently. "That would be lovely. I'd appreciate it."

"Well, I guess I'd better get home. We'll be having dinner soon. Thanks for the book. I don't read much, but I'm gonna start reading this one tonight."

Rose got up and they walked together towards the exit. "Oh, by the way," Dawn said, "what does that verse you wrote down say?"

"It says, 'God is our refuge and strength, an ever-present help in trouble.' God never lies. We know the Bible to be accurate and that verse helped me through some difficult times. I like to share it, since everyone—Christian or otherwise—will have trials in their lives, and just knowing we don't have to face them alone, helps."

"Wow. I wish I'd known it last year when my brother was in a car crash. I was scared he was gonna die. He's okay now though, thank God. My grandma prayed non-stop."

"Yes," Rose said as she patted Dawn's arm. "You can thank God for that."

"But what if he'd died?" she asked, her brows knit together.

"We can't question what happens in life. We don't have the thoughts of God, but we know there's purpose in everything, even if we can't understand it. I have my website listed in the back of the book, Dawn. You can always write to me with questions—and you will have them. I'll answer what I'm able to, but no one really has all the answers. Many will be answered in that little testament I gave you, though. Maybe you should start reading the Gospel of John. It's near the beginning."

"Okay. I'll read your book first, and then—"

"Actually, why not start with the Bible, and once you've read it through, you can start my book."

"If you think that would be better."

"I do."

Dawn reached over and embraced Rose. "I'm so glad I met you. Maybe when I learn to pray, I can pray for you and your daughter to meet someday."

"Thank you," Rose said softly, unable to say more. She watched as the girl walked down the sidewalk to her car.

"Yes," she said in a low whisper, "God had at least one purpose for me to take this trip. Thank you, Jesus."

Chapter Twelve

Paul checked his phone frequently to see if he'd missed any calls. Nothing. He stopped work on time for a change and went home to see his parents and grab some home-cooked food. Now that Hazel had stopped providing them with good meals, he, Ben and Jeremiah had to fend for themselves. Sometimes, they ordered pizza or Chinese food to be delivered, or picked up hoagies at the grocery store. Tonight, they had each gone their own way.

Jeremiah still kept his distance from Paul, even though they conversed about the business.

Since the evening when Paul stopped by to see Deborah and Ebenezer and ended up running into Hazel, he avoided visiting them. He missed his friends though, and figured he'd just make sure Hazel's buggy wasn't visible before stopping by again. Perhaps he'd run by after supper.

Two of his brothers were at the family farm when he arrived home, along with their wives and children, so he spent time catching up on their lives. No one mentioned Martha, which surprised him. He wondered if they were somewhat disappointed that he hadn't stuck with Hazel, since his family was close to hers. It couldn't be helped.

He was about to leave, when he felt his phone vibrate in his pocket. He stepped into the hallway and glanced. It was Martha! Quickly, he yelled good-bye and nearly ran to his waiting buggy. On the fifth ring, he answered.

"Martha!"

"*Jah*, it's me. How are you?"

"Not so *gut*, that's for certain."

"*Nee*. Me neither." There was silence.

"How's your *mamm*?" Paul asked, to be polite.

"She starts chemo in a few days. She's dreading it, but she keeps cheerful."

"Are you doing much cooking?"

"*Jah*, though *Mamm* likes to do it, when she can." Silence.

They both began talking at once and ended up laughing awkwardly. "Okay, you first, Martha," Paul said.

"*Nee*. You go first."

"I guess I was wondering if you had plans to visit with Deborah anytime soon," Paul said.

"Not really. How about you? Planning any trips— anywhere?"

"Now that you mention it, I was thinking about going into Lancaster."

"*Jah?* What's in Lancaster?"

"Well, nearby, there happens to be a beautiful girl whom I want to marry someday, if she'll have me."

Martha burst into tears. "You still care?"

"Oh, honey, of course I do. I can't turn off love like you did those switches at your apartment. Please don't cry. It makes me feel terrible-bad."

"Why haven't you written?" she asked through her tears.

"You know I hate to write."

"*Ach.* I should have written to you, I guess. You can't believe how many times I began a letter, but I never seemed to know the right words. We need to see each other in person." She sniffed and reached in her pocket for a tissue.

"I totally agree. How about tomorrow?"

"Are you serious?"

"*Jah*, I even checked with Skip Davis. He said anytime."

"Oh, my goodness! I can't believe it. What time can you be here? Oh, I forgot, I have to take my *dawdi* at noon to the doctor's. He has diabetes, Paul."

"Oh no. I'm sorry to hear that. Maybe your *Aenti* Liz can take him for you."

"Maybe. I can ride over first thing in the morning and ask her. And then she can take *Mamm* for her last radiation treatment and we'll spend the whole day together!"

"That would be wonderful-*gut*. You can plan where you want to go. Maybe we should take a picnic lunch somewhere. It's supposed to go into the mid-seventies."

"I know. It's been beautiful here."

"*Jah*, and here, though I've been working so many hours lately, I hardly get a chance to enjoy it."

"Paul, it's going to be okay…with us. Isn't it?"

"Of course. We just need to be together more often. Look for me around ten. You're sure it'll be okay with your family?"

"I'm sure it will be. They must be tired of seeing my grouchy face."

"You could never be grouchy."

"Oh, *jah*! For sure, I can be. Watch out!" she teased and they laughed at the same time.

After she got off the phone, Martha raced home to tell her parents to expect a visitor. But there in the driveway was another visitor—Daniel. She'd have to tell him to stay away from their house for the next couple of days. She sure didn't need another fight!

Daniel walked over to the buggy and began to unharness her horse as he told her he wanted to stop by to see how her mother was doing.

"Daniel, is that the only reason you stop so frequently? Really?"

He gave her a crooked grin. "There may be other reasons."

"It's pretty obvious you still have hopes we can get together. You know how I feel."

"Do I? I think there's a certain person who may be cooling off. I sure wouldn't be gone as much as your boyfriend is—if you were my girl."

"He's coming tomorrow, so I hope you have the decency to stay away the next few days."

They headed for the horse stables, Daniel carrying the harnessing as Martha led the horse. "Don't worry, I'll avoid stopping for a couple days, if that's what you want."

"It is."

"You going to tell him we see each other?"

"It's not necessary, after all there's nothing going on between us."

"There was."

"He knows all that. He also knows I love only one man."

"I guess I should be happy you've found a guy, but I sure do wish it was me."

"You're sweet to say that, Daniel, and I'm sorry to disappoint you, but I've always been honest about it. I've never led you on."

"That's true. I know I made a terrible mistake to force a kiss on you that day. I'm real sorry. It's not like me."

"It's okay. Water under the bridge. And I am fond of you, in a friend kind of way."

"If you do marry Paul, can we continue to be friends?"

"That might be hard. I don't think Paul would be too excited about that."

"Well, you won't be around here anyway, so it probably won't come up. I'll miss you. I just like being with you, Martha."

She nodded and swallowed hard. He sure didn't need to see his effect on her. He'd misread it for certain.

"Do you want to come in and stay awhile?" she asked.

"I don't think so. I already saw your folks. And now I've seen you." They stopped walking after they reached the stable. After he hung the harnessing on the peg, he turned to face her. "If you ever change your mind, just let me know. I'd marry you in a heartbeat."

"*Danki.* That's nice of you to say."

He took her hands in his and leaned over, kissing her forehead gently, then turned and left for his buggy. He didn't look back. If he had, he would have seen her tears.

She opened the gate to the pasture and watched as Chessy went to greet one of the work horses. Animals had it easy. Why was life so complicated for humans?

Chapter Thirteen

Martha was surprised that her mother did not seem particularly pleased about Paul's upcoming visit, after all the things she had told her sister about wanting their marriage to take place. She got the distinct impression that both her parents were disturbed by the news, though nothing was actually said. She, on the other hand, was excited beyond words. Certainly, all the doubts would be erased once they were together again.

The next morning, she gave her hair an extra shampooing and trimmed her neglected fingernails. It would be fun to add some polish for color like she had once when she lived as an English girl in her rented apartment, but it would never do here in this strict Amish community.

Right after an early breakfast, she took the open buggy over to her aunt's house and asked her about taxiing her grandfather to his appointment and then taking care of her mother's trip for her last radiation treatment. Though her father was more than willing to drive them, his chores had mounted up and two of his neighbors were going to help with the cultivating all week to help him catch up. One of Lizzy's sons had spent the previous week giving him a hand as well.

When she told Lizzy about Paul's upcoming visit and why it would be helpful if she could take over, her aunt's brows rose. "Well, I'm glad you're going to get things worked out with that young man—one way or the other. I'll be happy to take my *daed* and your *mamm* to their appointments. I noticed you've been downhearted lately and I finally know the reason. Now you be strong, Martha. Paul needs to know how important it is for you to be near your family."

"It might work out best for me to move though, *Aenti* Liz. Please understand that I haven't made up my mind yet."

"Dear girl, you see how much you're needed here. How can you possibly think of moving so far?"

"But it's not like I'd be going to Ohio, the way you all left your family years ago."

Liz took hold of her niece's hands and squeezed them as she looked directly into her eyes. "We did that for you, Martha. Entirely for you. Now maybe it's up to you to think of us."

"But you sounded like you wanted it to work out for Paul and me."

"And I do. If he loves you enough, he'll move to Lancaster County. I'm sure he would do that for you."

"He has a partnership. I don't even know if he could legally get out of it, and a house for us. A really cute house with several bedrooms. I'm not sure I want him to leave all that. Mightn't he resent me later on, if he gave all that up, just for me?"

Lizzy dropped Martha's hands and shook her head.

"There is a lot to think about, for sure. I don't envy you. So much to consider."

"I think a lot will depend on how *Mamm* does with her cancer. I hope she's cured and won't feel the need to have me with her all the time. She's been encouraging us to marry. Is she just pretending?"

"Nee, she wants to see you happy, but even though she acts brave and says you should do whatever you want, I think down deep, she's scared to have you leave her. You've always been more than a *dochder* to her—a friend, and companion as well."

"Paul would say that's not normal."

"Would he now? Has he said things like that?"

"Maybe not in those words, but he thinks she should manage real *gut* with the rest of the family near her."

"Oh, Martha, maybe he's right." She lowered her eyes. "I love your *mudder* and you so much, I just don't always think right. Maybe I'm being a *dummkopf.*"

"*Nee, Aenti*, I understand. Truly. You know I love you very much, too."

"Well, things will work out in the end. They always do, if we listen to *Gott*. Now, you run along while I get ready to pick up my parents. And don't worry about a thing. I should take over some of the trips for you, anyway. I just hadn't given it a thought. I guess none of us have realized how much you've taken on since you've been home. We take you for granted, I'm afraid."

"I want to be useful. You haven't asked me to do anything I wouldn't have wanted to do myself. I've had time to think about my being adopted, *Aenti*, and what that whole thing meant. It must have been difficult for the girl who gave birth to me to make that decision. I'm so thankful she did, though. If she hadn't, I never would have been part of this wonderful family. I believe *Gott* had his hand on every one of us."

"Do you ever wonder what your birth mother is like? Would you be able to forgive her for giving you away?"

"Oh, mercy, yes. She did something very unselfish, and she was so young. Do I ever wonder about her? I guess, occasionally, but I'm not going to try to find her. I'm happy just the way things are, and I wouldn't want to upset *Mamm*."

"*Jah*, it might. I don't know. We don't talk about it. Well, run along and get ready for Paul, and I hope you have a nice time together."

"*Aenti* Liz, can I have that photograph of my Italian father?"

"Oh, *jah*. I'll give it to you. Wait a minute while I find it." She went into the front room and came back with the picture in a yellowish envelope.

Martha took it and placed it in her pocket. "I don't think I'll look at it until after Paul leaves. I don't know how it's going to affect me and I have enough on my mind right now."

"I understand. Are you anxious about seeing Paul again?"

"I'm a little nervous, but more excited than anything. We're going on a picnic when he gets here. I have to go make sandwiches and frost the cake before he gets here."

"Come give me a hug first, Marty-girl," her *aenti* said, using her pet name. Martha went over and they embraced. "I know you'll do the right thing," her aunt whispered. "Whatever that is, your *mamm* will be just fine, to be sure. She's a strong woman and her main concern is your happiness."

"I know," Martha said, her voice shaking slightly.

She left then, waved to her uncle, who was feeding the chickens, and made her way home, more anxious than ever to spend time with the man she loved.

Jeremiah was surprised to see Hazel pull up in her buggy and park in front of the display room. He could see her from the work area as she climbed down. Such a lovely *maed*. Oh, that she still cared for him. He reached the door first and opened it for her.

"Hi, Jeremiah," she said, smiling, so sweetly, his heart leaped.

"Well, hi! What brings you here?" he asked as he led her in.

"It's been a while since I've stopped by." Her eyes darted about the room, giving him the distinct impression that she was looking for someone. She nodded over at Ben, who grunted a greeting, but continued staining a cabinet on the other side of the workroom.

"*Nee*, if you're looking for Paul, he went to see Martha for a couple days."

"Oh, that's to be expected, I guess. But tell me how you've been, Jeremiah?" she asked, taking a seat at the end of the work table, without waiting for an invitation.

"Pretty lousy, if you really want to know." He moved a side chair over to the table and sat where they could speak without straining their voices.

"I'm sorry. It's my fault, ain't?"

"I guess you could say that."

"I've given this whole thing a lot of thought, Jeremiah, and maybe I spoke too quickly about my feelings. Sometimes a girl really doesn't know how she feels about a man."

"You seemed pretty sure, I'm real certain of that."

"Well, unless you're dating someone else, I think maybe we should try again."

"I don't want to be hurt."

"Sometimes you have to take a chance."

"I don't know." He pulled on his suspenders and leaned on the back two legs of his chair. He looked over at her, but remained silent.

"I brought you something," she said, reaching into her apron pocket.

His eyes lit up. *"Jah?"*

"I made fudge this morning." She handed over a small *toot.*

He peeked in and grinned. "Wow! Is it made with…"

"Yup. Peanut butter. Your favorite."

"So, you really didn't come hoping to find Paul."

"Nee, Jeremiah. I came to see you."

"Tell me you no longer care about Paul."

She nodded.

"Please say the words, Hazel, but only if you mean them."

"I care about you, Jeremiah. That's all I can say at this point."

"I guess that's going to have to be enough for now."

"When I can say more, I will. I want it to work out for us."

"Then I'll stop over tonight and we can go for a buggy ride, okay?" A grin spread across his entire face.

"I'll be ready. Just give me a time."

"Seven?"

"Seven, it is." She rose and left without another word. He stood by the window, watching. When she got into her open buggy, she looked over at the large front display window and caught Jeremiah's eye. She waved as she coaxed her horse to make a turn.

Jeremiah thought of nothing else the entire time he worked. He tucked the bag of fudge in his pocket, not even offering any to Ben. It was way too special to give away.

The two-hour trip from Lewistown to Paradise seemed longer than usual. Paul and his driver talked about everything from the weather to politics. It helped somewhat, but the time still dragged on.

Finally, as the car pulled into the drive of the Troyer's farm, Paul saw Martha walking over from the side yard to greet him. The family dog, Spunky, trotted along beside her, but when he caught sight of Paul, he bounded over and leaped up. Paul laughed as he patted him on his head and told him to settle down. When he looked up, Martha was standing a few feet from them, her eyes displaying joy at his presence. He wanted so much to grab her and twirl her around, but he could see her father working the closest field. Melvin had two of the local men helping him with the cultivating. Though Melvin didn't stop to come over, he waved to Paul, and Paul waved back.

"Where's your *mamm*?" he asked.

"She's resting up for her visit to the hospital this afternoon. My grandparents are at the doctor's with my *aenti*. It's just you and me."

"Are you sure?" he asked, his eyes twinkling.

"Well, I might be more sure if we were at the brook. I made us a picnic lunch, just like you wanted."

"I'm glad. You look wonderful-*gut*, Martha."

"*Jah*? You, too. I've missed you."

"It's been hard."

"We should have written to each other," she added. "But forget the past. Come with me and we'll get some bottles of water and the basket of food. I'm starving."

"It's only eleven," he said walking beside her, without touching her.

"But I didn't have breakfast. I tried, but I was too excited."

"I think you're thinner."

"I lost a few pounds, I guess. You look *gut* though."

"I never weigh myself, but my trousers seem a little looser."

"I made spice cake this morning with cream cheese frosting. You can have two pieces now and then take some home with you tomorrow."

"Oh, I was hoping to stay two nights."

"Really? Wonderful! I'll tell *Mamm*."

Once they placed the food and water in a woven basket, Martha reached for an old worn quilt she'd folded on a chair, and Paul picked up the basket as they prepared to leave.

Sarah walked in as they headed for the back door. "Oh, I didn't hear you come in," Sarah said, looking over. "Are you going on your picnic, Martha?"

"*Jah.* I should have called up to you, but I didn't want to disturb you."

"It's okay. Well, have fun. It's a beautiful spring day," she added.

"Paul can stay two nights, *Mamm*."

"Oh. Sure."

"You're looking pretty *gut*, Mrs. Troyer," Paul said as they headed for the door.

"Better than I feel," she remarked.

"I'm sorry to hear that."

"*Ach.* Can't be helped. Hopefully, in time, I'll get rid of this cancer. It's a battle."

"*Jah*, for sure it is, but you are a strong person. I know you'll be fine someday."

"Hopefully," she said as she went to heat up the early coffee. "I'll be home later. You may have to cook supper, Martha, if I'm too tired. I did make stew for your father for his dinner. I guess he can heat it up if you're not home. There's enough for the other men, if they stay."

"I'm sure he can do that, *Mamm*."

"*Jah*, he may have to get used to doing things for himself."

Martha and Paul exchanged glances. It wasn't her mother's normal behavior. She was not usually so negative.

Once out of sight, Paul reached for Martha's free hand and squeezed it as they walked across a field and made their way through bramble to the edge of a narrow stream, which meandered cheerfully over smoothly rounded rocks. They stopped and laid everything down on a clearing at the side of the brook. Then Paul took Martha in his arms and kissed her, first gently, and then passionately on her lips.

When he pulled back, she opened her eyes and smiled. "I've missed you."

He nodded. "It's been a nightmare. I didn't know what to do. I wanted to talk to you, but…"

"I'm sorry. I let the battery die, I'm afraid, and then… well, let's not talk about it. It's over and we're together again and everything is *gut*. Right?"

"*Jah*, my love will never change."

After another amorous kiss, they spread the quilt on

the ground and sat a few minutes watching the rippling water before taking out their lunch. "Looks *gut*," Paul said as she handed him a wrapped sandwich on home-made bread. "Chicken salad?"

"Tuna," she said, grinning.

"I like that, too," he said, smiling back.

"And we can eat the cake now or later."

"Maybe later."

After finishing their sandwiches, Paul patted the ground next to him. "Why don't you come closer? I want to hold you." She moved over and laid her head against his chest as he surrounded her with his arms.

"We do need to talk, Martha. About the future."

"I know."

"You need to finish the instructions for the baptism, otherwise we'll have to wait another year."

"I think it will be a year anyway, Paul. I have to wait and see how my *mudder* does."

He nodded. "I've figured out that with the money coming in now, you could hire a driver and visit your family often. Maybe even a day a week."

"Oh."

"I thought you'd be pleased." His embrace concluded as she sighed and lifted her head.

Then Martha sat back. "It might work out, until the *kinner* come along."

"Hopefully, by then, your *mamm* would be all better and they could visit us. I'd be happy to pay for any expense."

"I doubt my *daed* would allow that. Even though he's Amish, he has some pride."

Paul placed his hands around his drawn knees. "Are you changing your mind about moving?"

"I've never made up my mind. I have to ask you something, Paul."

"Ask away," he said, looking over with drawn lips.

"Would you consider moving to Lancaster County and starting your own business here?"

"Martha, I hope you're kidding. Do you realize how fortunate I am to be in a partnership already? And be purchasing the business, which incidentally has a house for us? It's almost unheard of at my age. I'd have to start all over."

"But if it meant making your wife happy?"

He shook his head. "I would think my wife would be happier if she knew she would be provided for real *gut*, and that her husband was fulfilling his dream."

"In other words, it's my moving, or it's over?"

"Martha, Martha, I never said that."

"It sure sounds like you mean that though. My *mudder* could be dying, you know. She'd be heartbroken, if I left her at this awful time."

"But she could live another thirty years. It's not like they don't have hopes of curing her."

"It's serious, Paul. It's not a simple case. She starts chemo now. They don't do that unless they're concerned. It has spread, you know."

"Martha, isn't it true that *Gott* is in charge? Isn't it His will that will be done? Regardless of what man wants?"

"What does that have to do with anything?" Tears formed and one rolled down her cheek.

"I guess what I'm trying to say is, whether you're at home with her or away as my bride, *Gott* is in charge. You're staying here won't change that."

"You really don't understand, Paul. She should be

surrounded by her family—people who love her, especially if she doesn't have much time left."

"I guess I understand." He reached for a paper napkin and wiped her cheeks. "Don't cry, Martha. I don't want you upset. Let me think all this through and pray about it. You're asking a lot of me, but I don't want to lose you."

"Maybe if you agree to stop pushing me for marriage for another year, we'll know more about the outcome. If *Mamm* is cured, things would be easier for me to move away."

"A year seems like forever, but I guess it really isn't. I'll try to be more patient. I've just been so excited about the house and having you there with me, I guess I need to relax."

"We can see each other more often, though, Paul. I want to visit with Deborah and her family. I'll try to come one night, maybe even next week."

His eyes lit up. "I'll pay the driver."

"I have some money from working. I'd pay for it myself."

"Oh, do I hear a little *hochmut* from my Martha?"

"It's not pride. Well, maybe." She smiled. "Anyway, I'll pay."

"Now let's not spoil the rest of our time together. I'm dying for some of that cake now."

She reached over and pulled out a huge piece wrapped in plastic wrap and gave it to him on a paper plate with a plastic fork. "You'd better say you like it," she said with a wink. "And that it's even better than Hazel's."

A wave of guilt nearly overwhelmed him at the men-

tion of Hazel's name. Goodness, why was he so confused? Surely, he didn't still have feelings for Hazel.

After one mouthful, he nodded. "Best I ever had,"
he said, feeling that to be the safest response.

Chapter Fourteen

The rest of their day together went well. They merely avoided certain topics, which included Daniel, Hazel, or a date for the wedding. Of course, where they'd live was definitely off limits.

Later, her grandparents joined the family for supper. When asked about his visit with the doctor, her grandfather told them the diabetes could be controlled with medication, but it might take time to get his system balanced. He seemed reassured by the doctor's explanations.

Then Sarah remarked she was glad to be finished with the radiation treatments, even though it meant the chemo would begin again. That was the extent of the family conversations. No one asked Paul how his business was faring, which annoyed Martha, though she made no mention of it to Paul when they were alone later. After their uneventful supper, Paul suggested a buggy ride, which Martha agreed to immediately. It would be pleasant to get away alone again. There had been a definite strain throughout the entire meal.

* * *

As the horse trotted along the country road, Paul proposed they go into town and stop at their favorite ice cream shop. Martha teased him about gaining all his weight back in one day, but she loved ice cream and agreed to his idea most willingly. When they arrived, Paul secured the reins to a hitching post and they went in, sat at their favorite table and waited for service.

Dawn Hanson looked over at the newly arrived couple. It was Martha Troyer and the young man she usually came in with. Excited, she nodded over and nearly ran to the drawer where she'd tucked the letter from the nice lady author, who claimed to be Martha's birth mother. Hopefully, Martha would not be upset to receive it—especially in front of the handsome Amish boyfriend.

She placed the letter in her pocket and made her way over to the waiting couple to take their order. She decided to wait for things to slow down before giving Martha the letter. She greeted the couple and Martha asked how she'd been. After the usual response, Dawn asked what they'd like.

They each decided on a sundae. Martha had her usual vanilla ice cream with chocolate syrup and whipped cream, and Paul asked for butter pecan ice cream, topped with butterscotch sauce. Dawn went back to the counter to fill the order. She had two other tables, but they'd already been served. After leaving off their checks, she came back to Martha's table and set their sundaes in front of them. Then she removed the envelope from her pocket.

"Excuse me, Martha, but I wanted to give you this,"

she said as she laid it on the table next to Martha, who looked up rather bewildered.

"For me?"

"Yup. It's real important. A lady who writes books came in here and asked if I knew anyone with your last name. When I told her I knew you, she...well, you'll see when you read the letter, I'm sure. I hope it will make you happy." Dawn avoided looking over at Paul. It was an awkward moment.

Martha picked up the envelope and stared at it. Then she looked over at Paul.

"Aren't you going to read it?" he asked.

Dawn shook her head towards Martha. "Maybe you should wait," she said cryptically.

Martha studied her expression, trying to decipher the meaning behind the odd words. "Okay, I'll wait. *Danki*. I mean—thank you, Dawn."

"It's okay. I hope it makes you happy." Martha watched as Dawn turned and went over to the register where a young woman was waiting to pay.

Paul put his spoon down. "Aren't you curious?"

"Very."

"So, open it, or is it from a secret admirer?"

"Don't be silly. I'd rather wait, though. It might be serious."

"It sounded like it would be something *gut*, from what that girl said."

"Oh, what a day. I can't take anything else right now. I'm too filled with weird emotions."

"Martha, have I upset you?" He leaned over and put his hand close to hers, without touching it.

"I can't explain what's going on inside me. I don't even know. I'm so mixed up. I'm worried about *Mamm*, lonely for you, curious about this, and I even have my father's picture, which I haven't had the courage to look at yet. I just wish life would be easier."

"I could make it easier for you, if you become my wife soon."

"See? You see how you make things worse?" She burst into tears. "I have to leave."

"Martha, you're acting so strange. Okay, go out and I'll pay for this. I don't know what's going on with you. My *daed* always said women were hard to understand."

Martha slipped out of the ice cream shop without saying anything further to Dawn. She climbed into her seat and allowed the tears to flow. Good thing she'd taken a couple paper napkins with her. A few moments later, Paul appeared. He climbed in and immediately drew the reins and clucked for the horse to back up.

Martha stopped crying and blew her nose. For several minutes, neither of them spoke. Then Paul broke the silence. "I guess you weren't ready for me to come visit. I just seem to make things worse."

"Not true."

"But look at you. You're a bit of a mess, Martha. You have to get hold of yourself. You're not a young teenager anymore."

"You really don't understand, do you, Paul? You don't seem to have any feelings."

"Of course, I do. I want to understand you, but it wonders me. Even the letter. Why didn't you read it?"

"Maybe I need to be alone. I have a feeling I know who it's from."

He glanced over and questioned with his eyes. "Do you want to share with me?"

"Why don't you pull over at the grove near the farm

when you get there, and we'll read it together? I do want to share things with you, Paul, but you seem to be upset with me all the time."

"Not true, Martha. I'm just sad to see you like this."

They finally arrived at the grove and he pulled the horse to a stop. Then he turned in his seat and waited for Martha to read the letter. She removed it from the envelope and began.

"Dear Martha,
You don't really know me, but I am the woman
who gave birth to you twenty years ago."

Martha looked over at Paul. He reached over for her hand. "Go on, Martha."

"Not a day has passed, that I haven't thought
of you and wondered how you were doing. I'd
made an agreement when your family adopted
you to stay out of your life, which I have done—
until now. I figure you are old enough to handle
it, if we should ever have an opportunity to meet.
It is my greatest desire to see you in person. To
get to know you, at least a little. I hope you have
forgiven me for giving you to another to raise."

Martha's voice trembled and she found it difficult to read. "Please Paul, read it to me. I feel like I'm choking."

He took the letter carefully from her shaking hand, and continued, speaking softly as he read.

"If you decide not to pursue this any further, I
will understand, but I am hoping—and praying—

*that you will contact me. I live in Ohio, but I can
travel anytime, since I'm a writer and can take
my computer wherever I go. I write Amish books
under a different name and am actually doing a
book signing in Lancaster before I go back home.
I'll write my address and my phone number down,
just in case you should decide to try to reach me.*

"In sincere love,
"Rose Esh"

He looked over at Martha, who had her head covered with her hands. Her body was shaking. He set the
letter aside, moved from his seat and knelt beside her,
surrounding her gently with his arms. "It's okay, honey.
Don't cry. You don't have to get in touch with her, if it's
too painful for you."

"Oh, Paul, I knew it was from her. I just knew it.
Of all times—I'm just not ready for any more stress. I
can't take it."

"I can write back to her for you, if you want."

"I can't think about it now. Maybe later. All these
years. Why now?"

"I guess she stayed away because of their agreement."

"Jah." Martha tried to calm down as Paul held her
and kissed her cheek.

"I don't think you should tell your *mamm*, do you?"
he said softly.

"Nee. I won't. I have my *daed*'s picture in my pocket.
Do you want to see it?"

"I already saw it, remember? But I want to be with
you when you look at it. Now would be a *gut* time,

Martha. Maybe it will help to face all this while I'm with you."

"Jah." She moved away slightly and reached into her apron pocket. She withdrew the envelope and removed the photograph. The light had begun to diminish as dusk was approaching, but she had enough light to note the features of the handsome young Italian man smiling back at her from the picture. She could almost see her own smile. His dark wavy hair and deep brown eyes explained so much. Would she ever meet him? Did she even want to?

At this moment, she grieved for the young couple. How tragic not to be able to raise your child, conceived in love, though carelessly—without thought; a child who had been brought into this world through no choice of her own. What would her life have been like, if they had married and kept her? Would she have been raised in Italy?

"Why didn't they marry, Paul?"

"Her parents were very strict Amish. They were ashamed, of course, to have their daughter have a child out of wedlock. This was a far better solution for them and in the end—better for you, Martha. Look how much you love your family, and they love you."

"He's a nice-looking young man, don't you think? He looks like a pleasant person, as well."

"Jah, I'm sure he was a charmer. Maybe after your *mamm* gets better, you can talk to her about all this. You may want to write to this Rose lady at some point. She sounds like she's nice."

"I kind of wish I'd known before and could have sneaked into the bookstore when she signed her new book. Just to hear her talk and all."

"*Jah*, that might have been *gut*, but it didn't happen, so…"

"I know. So many turns in the road, *jah*?"

He nodded. "Life can be strange. I'm just thankful we met and fell in love, Martha. We can't let all this other stuff in life change our feelings. We have something special."

"You will think about what we talked about, won't you?"

"*Jah*, for sure. I need time to think things through, Martha. I want your happiness above all. It's just that you're so stressed out right now, we don't want to make the wrong choices. We have to look at the big picture."

"And we need to pray about it. Not that I haven't, but maybe we should pray together."

"That's a *gut* idea. Take my hand again, sweetheart." She reached across and they clasped their hands together and bowed their heads.

"Dear *Gott* in heaven," Paul began. "We want to do what's right with our lives. You know how much we love each other, and we want to marry when it's the proper time. Please give us wisdom and help us make the best decisions. Be with Martha's *mudder* and make her well again. Please make Martha strong enough to handle whatever comes her way and help me to be more understanding and give me much more patience." He stopped and then Martha added a few words.

"*Gott*, be with my other *mudder* as well and help her to not feel too guilty and upset about giving me up for adoption. And if You want me to, help me to write back some day and even meet her—if it's Your will. Keep Paul and me together and take away some of this pain I have." She stopped and together they whispered, "Amen."

Her tears had ceased. She took the letter and picture back from Paul and placed them in her pocket. Then they started back to the house, the clip-clopping of the horse's hooves a comforting sound of normalcy upon their ears. Life would go on, and God would give them the strength they'd need to face whatever lay ahead.

Chapter Fifteen

Deborah and her husband, Ebenezer, wrapped towels around the triplets after bathing them and made sure the boys were thoroughly dry before helping them with their pajamas. Then he took them to their bedroom.

Their twin girls were already settled down for the night. It would be nice to have an hour or so to themselves, Deborah thought, as she cleaned the ring out of the tub with a scrubbing sponge.

She heard Ebenezer, in the next room, telling the boys to settle down for prayers. What a change in him since he came to realize he was needed. Trying to raise five young children by herself was almost impossible, given their strong wills and temperaments. It was wonderful her sisters, Hazel and Wanda, came frequently to help out, but they couldn't be there every day. Her mother wasn't much help, since she spent time with the other grandchildren.

When she was expecting the twin girls and during the early days of their lives, she had leaned heavily on Martha. What a wonderful help she'd been. She missed her, as a friend, as much as a helper.

After the boys were settled down for the night, she and Ebenezer went downstairs and sat together on their lumpy sofa. He put his arm around her and kissed her cheek. "Tired?"

"Ain't I always?"

He patted her expanding abdomen with his free hand. "You're popping pretty *gut*. Maybe you'll have twins again," he said with a grin.

"Oh, please don't even think it. One at a time would be real nice from now on."

"We don't have much say in the matter."

"*Nee*, but after this one is born, I may need a little time before getting in a family way again."

"I'll try to stay away from you, Debbie, but you're such a cutie. You're asking a lot of a man." He reached over and removed her *kapp* and searched for one of her hairpins.

Deborah laughed and poked her husband under his rib. "Goodness, what would the bishop say if he heard you talk like that?"

"The bishop's wife didn't have eleven *kinner* all by herself, you know."

There was a knock on the back door and then they heard it open.

"I didn't hear a buggy pull up, did you?" he asked, rising from the sofa.

"*Nee*, but we just came down."

Paul walked into the room. "Oh, I guess I'm too late to play with the boys."

"*Jah*, don't talk too loud," Ebenezer said, putting his index finger to his lips to silence his friend. "We just got them settled down."

"Did I interrupt something?" Paul asked, looking over at Deborah, who was reaching for her *kapp*.

"*Nee*, that's fine," she responded, replacing the *kapp* over her messed hair. "So, what's going on in your life, Paul? We hardly ever see you anymore."

"I just got back a couple days ago from visiting Martha. That's the latest news."

"Oh, how is her *mudder* doing?" Deborah asked.

"I can't really say. She's finished with radiation treatments and now she's getting chemo."

"How's Martha handling things?" Deborah asked.

"She's okay, I guess. Pretty emotional though." He proceeded to fill them in on the letter she received from her birth mother, and then he told them about her decision to stay at home, at least for a year before marrying.

"I understand how she feels," Deborah said. "She'll feel freer to move away from her family, once she knows her *mudder* will be okay."

"And if she ain't?" Ebenezer put in.

"We can't think that way, Eb," Deb said, glaring over. "Think positive."

"You have to be realistic," he countered.

"I think all this treatment is going to work," Paul said. "Martha would like me to move to Lancaster when we marry."

"That's not going to work," Ebenezer said. "You have your business—even a nice house. She wouldn't be that far away from her family."

"I know all that, but she's very close to her *mudder*."

"Maybe too close," Deborah said. "I mean, she shouldn't expect you to give up all you've worked for. You have a wonderful business already established. I hate to say it, because you know I love Martha, but it seems selfish to expect you to be the one to move."

"Now, that's not up to us to say," Eb added.

"It's okay," Paul said. "Maybe you can talk to her about it, Deb. She wants to pay you a visit soon. She even thought in a week or so, though a lot will depend on how her *mudder* reacts to the chemo. I haven't talked to her since I left, so I don't know if she's gotten sick from it or not."

"You used to talk every night," Deb reminded him.

"It's hard, since she won't use the cell phone. Sometimes she's just too tired to go to the community phone."

"Her bishop is pretty strict, ain't?" Eb asked.

"*Jah*, that's another thing I don't like about moving there. It's hard to go backwards. I mean, I like having my cell phone, and he's really against it."

"Even if you had a business?"

"That I don't know. He'd probably allow a phone for business. I'd have to find out."

"So, you're actually considering it? Moving?" Eb asked.

"I don't want to lose her. I really love her. You know that."

"Maybe it's none of my business," Deb said quietly, "but I talked to Hazel and she told me what happened between you two."

Paul's brows hit his bangs. *So, she'd talked.*

Eb looked over at his wife. "What happened? You didn't tell me anything."

"It was a strange moment," Paul started. "I feel terrible, if I led her on."

"What did you do?" Eb asked, leaning forward.

"They kissed, Eb," Deb said.

"Holy mackerel! Why would you do that, if you're in love with Martha?"

"*Gut* question. One I can't really answer."

"She also said you thought you might be in love with two women."

"Did I say that?"

"I guess. Hazel doesn't lie. I know she's trying to get over you though. She told me she's going to go out with Jeremiah again."

"I hope it works out for them," Paul said.

"You really mean it, Paul?" Deb asked. "It sure sounded like you still had real feelings for Hazel, and she'd live anywhere in the world with you. I know for a fact, she still loves you."

"Then she shouldn't go dating Jeremiah," Eb said. "That just ain't fair to the man. He'd hurt pretty bad if she ended up with Paul here."

"That's not going to happen!" Paul said, with more confidence than he actually felt.

"You should spend more time with Hazel then," Eb said. "If anything is going to happen, you need to know soon. That's the only fair way to deal with this."

"I'm more confused than ever. Since that night when we kissed, I feel so guilty when I think of it. But sometimes when I'm with Martha, my mind goes to Hazel. When I'm with Hazel, I think about Martha. Maybe I should take off and start all over."

"You know that won't happen," Deb said. "I hope Martha pays us a visit soon. I'll have a nice talk with her and try to make her realize she might lose you, if she pushes the move too much."

"I don't know." Paul ran his hand through his straw-colored hair and rested his head on the back of the armchair.

"I bet you're sorry you stopped by," Eb teased.

"Well, you're two of my oldest friends. I value your opinion, but as far as dating Hazel? I couldn't do that to Martha or Jeremiah."

"You need to find out before you take the step to marry. It's way too important to end up marrying the wrong girl," Eb said. "Talk to Jeremiah and tell him what's going on."

"Whoa. That would be real hard. I don't want to hurt him. I don't want to hurt anyone and it looks like someone is going to be unhappy with me, no matter what I do."

"*Jah*, you're right about that, Paul," Deb said. "You got yourself in a pickle, if you ask me."

A voice came from upstairs. "Is that *Onkel* Paul?" came little Mark's voice.

"Uh oh. You'd better give the boys hugs quick-like, or we're gonna end up with three wild kids," Ebenezer said to Paul.

Paul rose quickly and went up to give out hugs and ended up reading *The Three Bears* for the umpteenth time. His mind was not on bears, however. The faces of two lovely Amish girls danced in his mind as his soul felt tormented.

One morning after receiving the chemo, Martha could hear her mother vomiting yet again in the bathroom. She stood by the door until her mother stopped retching. "*Mamm*, do you need help?"

"You can come in now. I think I'm done."

Martha opened the door and found her mother kneeling by the toilet. "I hoped I wouldn't be sick to my stomach."

"We need to talk to the doctor and see if they can give you something, *Mamm*."

"I'm taking something already, but it don't seem to help."

"Then you need something stronger. I'll go over to the phone today and call the doctor."

"Martha, maybe you should use the cell phone. I kept the one we took away from you."

"It would need charging, besides *Daed* would be upset."

"I'll talk to him about it. Maybe he can speak to the bishop and see if he'll make an exception. So many times, I've needed to talk to someone about my health problems. If something happened at night…well, I wouldn't want anyone going out in the dark. Too many accidents with our Amish buggies."

"Even if he relents, I'd still have to get it charged up. *Mamm*, I may as well tell you, I have another one, too. Paul bought it for me, but I haven't wanted to use it, knowing how *Daed* feels about it."

"You're a *gut* girl, Martha. The best. Paul shouldn't have bought you one, knowing how *Daed* feels."

"He was just trying to be helpful. We hardly ever talk anymore. It's too difficult between my being so tired at night and his working so many hours."

"*Ach.* It must be hard on you. Help me up, dear. I want to go lie down for a while. I'm real tired."

Martha helped her stand and held her arm while they walked down the hall to her mother's room. She straightened out the sheets and plumped up the pillows before her mother climbed in to rest.

"Danki, liebschdi."

Martha drew the shades and tiptoed out of the room. Her mother had already fallen asleep. She went into the bathroom and cleaned the toilet with cleanser and then flushed and added a few tablespoons of bleach to the bowl.

Perhaps it would be a good time to take the open buggy to the phone shed and call the doctor. Hopefully, they'd prescribe a stronger medicine for the nausea and vomiting. As she prepared to leave, her father came in through the kitchen door and nodded over. "How's your *mudder* doing?"

"Not gut. She just *kutzed* again. She's taking a nap." She explained about the phone call she wanted to make.

"I'll stay inside till you get home. I'll sit near the staircase in case she needs me. Poor woman. She's been through so much."

"I know. I put a meatloaf in a few minutes ago. Could you take it out when it's done, in case I'm delayed? It should be ready in an hour."

"*Jah*, I can do that."

"Do we need anything at the market that you know of, *Daed*?"

"You'd know better than me. Take your time, Martha. It's *gut* for you to get by yourself once in a while. You need a break. I can manage my meal if you're not home. I used to like to cook."

"Maybe I'll go to the open market and walk around a bit then. *Danki*." She went over and gave her father a hug. Poor man. This was just as tough on him. Plus, he had all the responsibilities of the farm. Too bad he'd never had sons.

* * *

It was a gorgeous day. Martha loved the month of May, but with everything going on in her life, she hadn't taken time to admire the beautiful flowers. The lilacs were nearly finished blooming, but she stopped at a bush next to the phone shed and breathed in the fragrant aroma. She sent a quick prayer of thanks to the great Creator as she went to the phone to call the doctor's office. The nurse who answered was able to talk to the doctor about a new prescription and she promised to call it in to the pharmacy as soon as they ended their call. That way, Martha could pick it up on her way home.

When she arrived at the market, she walked along the rows of vendors with their produce and homemade articles and stopped to speak to her many friends who worked there. She heard a man's voice call out her name, and when she turned, Daniel was standing right before her. "I didn't know you worked here," she said.

"Only when my friend, Moses, needs me. His wife is having a *boppli* right now, so I offered to help him out. Come back to the stand with me and we can talk. His *bruder* is coming soon to take over. Then I'm free. How about if we go out to lunch together."

The thought of relaxing with a friend was too tempting to refuse. "I'd love to, but I'll pay my own way."

"We'll see. How's your *Mamm* doing? I'm sorry I haven't been over in a while. I've been painting houses to make some extra money. I'm actually thinking of starting my own business. I like to paint. It's kind of relaxing. I'd still work the farm with my family, but it would bring in extra cash. What do you think?"

"It's a *gut* idea, Daniel. You're a hard worker."

"Now I am. I haven't always been, but I guess you

know that. I think I've finally grown up, Martha." He smiled over as a woman came to the stand and picked out two bags of fresh spinach. She paid him and left. He turned back to Martha. "What kind of food would you like? Chinese? Italian? Deutsch?"

"Oh, anything really."

"Then I'll take you out for spaghetti. I know you like that."

"I do! You remembered."

"Oh *jah*, you ate about a pound all by yourself the day we sat together at the group picnic."

"I pigged out, as my English friend would say."

"I see Moses's *bruder* coming now."

Martha knew Abraham from church. They exchanged greetings and he told them his sister-in-law had just given birth to a baby girl, who weighed in at nine pounds.

"She's a big *boppli*," Martha said. "How many *kinner* do they have now?"

"This makes it six. Five *maedel* and one *bu*."

After Abraham got his apron on, Daniel handed him the receipts along with the money box. Then he and Martha walked over to the section where the Amish parked their buggies. Martha made sure her horse had fresh water and then she followed Daniel over to his open buggy and climbed in.

They discussed the wonderful weather and he told her about the painting jobs he had lined up. They arrived at a small family-run Italian restaurant set back about a hundred yards from the road. There were several cars in the parking lot and Daniel pulled around back where there were hitching posts for the Amish. His was the only buggy so far. He secured his horse in the shadiest spot and reached over to help Martha out of the passenger side. He held her hand several instants longer than she thought necessary, which annoyed her. Not again. Maybe she shouldn't have accepted his invitation. He must have sensed she was uncomfortable because he kept his distance throughout the meal.

Martha ordered lasagna and Daniel decided on the chicken parmesan. Service was slow, which allowed them time to relax and converse. She noticed he had developed something of a sense of humor, and he kept her amused with stories of some of the events he'd experienced while painting people's homes.

Their salads arrived first, along with crispy Italian bread, fresh from the oven. Before reaching for their forks, they each lowered their heads and said a blessing silently over the food. Martha looked up first and observed Daniel's countenance. He was a nice-looking man with tidy blonde hair, just long enough to cover the lobes of his ears. He always looked clean, something she appreciated with Paul also. When he opened his eyes, he smiled over. His pale green eyes were so unusual, she felt slightly uncomfortable as she found it difficult to turn away.

"Do I have mud on my face?" he asked with a crooked grin forming.

"I'm sorry. I just never noticed what nice eyes you have. Pretty color."

"*Danki.* I got the color from my German grandmother. They gave her the nickname 'fern-eyes,' which she hated."

Martha laughed. "I don't think I'd like to be called that either."

"I wonder who you got your beautiful dark eyes from," he said.

"From my Italian father," she said without thought.

"Really. Interesting. I'd forgotten about your adoption. But your mother was Amish, right?"

"*Jah.* I may as well tell you. I heard from her recently. It would take too long to explain how she got in touch, but she'd like to meet me."

"So, when are you going to see her?"

"I'm not sure I am. I haven't decided yet."

"Huh. I'd think you'd be curious."

"In a way I am. It turns out she's a writer—of Amish books."

"Well, I guess she knows what she's writing about. Have you read any of them?"

"*Nee.* I may go to the library when I have a chance, and get one out to read."

"Amazing. After all these years. Do you have any bitterness towards her?"

"Not really."

The waiter returned with their entrees and refilled their empty water glasses. Then he removed their salad plates and went over to another table to get an order.

After a few bites, Martha raved about the food. "I wish I could cook like this."

"Someday, you will. It just takes practice."

"Do you still have your own apartment?"

He shook his head. "I moved back with my family, but it's rough at home lately. My father is so grouchy sometimes. I liked living alone better."

"Why did you move back?"

"Don't get mad at me. I moved back home because it was closer to you."

"Oh, Daniel. Not again." She put her fork down and folded her hands in her lap.

"Sorry I told you."

"You know there's no hope."

"Martha, you keep saying that, but I go by your place every day and I haven't seen Paul there except for the one time. What kind of guy would stay away from you just because of a job? I'd have to move to Lancaster if I knew you loved me. I hope you're not wasting your time on a guy who shows so little interest."

"It's not true! Paul loves me a whole lot. He works hard so he can provide *gut* for me when we marry. It will be worth it someday."

"Maybe he just likes to work."

"It's true he enjoys what he's doing, but it's still just a job."

"Where will you live if you marry?"

"I'm not sure."

"Have you talked about it yet? Don't wait until the wedding bells ring. You need to know now. Would he leave his business to come here?"

"Maybe. *Jah*, I'm sure he would, if I wanted him to."

"And you don't?"

"Daniel, it's none of your business. We're just friends, remember?"

"But I'm a friend who cares, Martha. I want you to be happy, and I'm not sure that guy's the one to make you happy. I think he's too self-centered."

"That's not fair! You barely know him! Why did you have to spoil our meal? I don't even feel like eating anymore. I'll take it home in a box. Maybe *Mamm* will want it."

"Oh, Martha. I'm sorry. Please, just calm down. I won't mention Paul again. Honest."

"It's too late. You've already ruined things. I won't be able to go anywhere with you again. It's too upsetting."

"Is it me? Or is there truth to what I say? Think about it, Martha. I won't bother you again, but until I know you're actually married and there's no more hope for me, I'm going to stay single and pray for us to one day get together. I really messed up before, but I wouldn't let it happen again. I realize now how much I really cared for you—and still do. Now we won't talk about this again. Just calm down and enjoy your meal. Please."

She sat silently watching as he spread butter on his bread. After a few minutes, she picked up her fork and proceeded to slowly eat her meal. Who was she angry with? Daniel? Paul? Or herself? She concentrated on the Italian music playing in the background. It seemed to hit a chord with her. Perhaps it was her Italian blood, but whatever it was, the music took her mind off her problems—temporarily, anyway.

Chapter Sixteen

No decisions were made about anything. The letter from her mother sat in her drawer alongside the picture of her father. She had not attempted to write back. Phone calls with Paul were still infrequent as the cell phone laid unused beside the letter. Martha had not seen Daniel since their lunch together, and she didn't discuss marriage with anyone. At least the new medication was helping her mother with the nausea. Though she was still tired most of the time, she was able to work alongside Martha in the kitchen and spend time with her own mother and sister on the quilt project.

Since things seemed to be under control, Martha approached her mother one afternoon about taking a couple days off and visiting with Deborah and her family. And of course, Paul lived right nearby.

Her mother encouraged Martha to take time off, though she didn't seem thrilled about Martha going to Lewistown.

"You'll be working harder there with all those *kinner*," she reminded her.

"I'm happy to help Deborah, but I need to spend

time with Paul, *Mamm*," Martha said, noting the expression on her mother's face. "After all, we're going to marry one day."

"*Jah*, of course," Sarah said. "Unless one of you changes your mind."

"I'm sure that's not going to happen."

"Honey, if you start to feel different towards Paul, better to face it before you marry. You don't want to make a mistake."

"You've never really liked Paul, have you?"

"He's a nice young man. I like him *gut* enough, but you don't seem so happy after you've been together. That ain't *gut*, you know."

"It's just hard being apart."

"Shouldn't make you get upset with each other."

"Well, I don't really want to talk about it, *Mamm*. I think I'll write to Deborah and see if next week would work out for me to visit."

"Are you going to surprise Paul?"

"Probably not. He'll need to work it out so he can take time off while I'm there."

"I thought he was the boss."

"He's a partner, but he takes his responsibility real serious-like and wouldn't want to leave Jeremiah with too much work."

"Mmm. I guess that's a *gut* thing then."

"Paul has wonderful-*gut* ethics, *Mamm*."

"I think Daniel does, too, now that he's grown up more. He stopped by when you were at *Aenti* Liz's yesterday. He told me about his new painting jobs."

"You didn't tell me he was by."

"He came to see me, so I guess I didn't think you'd be interested. Are you?"

"Uh, I guess not. Did he ask where I was?"

"Let me think. Did he? Mmm. *Jah*, I think so," she said, smiling over. "He told me you had lunch together recently. That was nice."

"He's still a friend."

"Oh, he's in love with you, for sure. He told me himself that he moved back home to be closer to you. How sweet."

"Oh *jah*, *super sweet*," Martha said mockingly.

"Now *dochder*, you sound so mean."

"Well, I wouldn't call him sweet."

"*Jah* well, perhaps that's the wrong word. Now, it's wondered me if you could brush out my hair while your *daed* is outside."

"Sure. Should we go up to your bedroom?"

"*Jah*, gut idea. Maybe the bathroom would be better. It's falling out real bad and I don't want to make a mess."

When they got upstairs, her mother stood in front of the sink and took off her *kapp*. Martha was shocked to see how thin it was. She'd always loved brushing it when she was younger. It had grown back in after her early bout with cancer and when Martha was a child, it was silky and golden blonde. Now the little that was left was almost totally grey.

Martha picked up the hairbrush and slowly went through the remaining strands. Each time she stroked it, she'd have to stop to remove the many strands caught in the bristles. She looked in the mirror. Her mother had tears streaming down her face. Her eyes looked back at Martha. "It's okay, dear. It will grow back. I guess I'm a vain Amish woman after all, but I hate this part. Even though I usually keep my *kapp* on, I know how bald I'm getting underneath it. I don't like your *daed* to see me this way."

"Oh, *Mamm*, goodness, it's to be expected. No one would think a thing of it—least of all *Daed*."

"It will grow back, don't you think?"

"Of course." She laid the brush aside and surrounded her mother with her arms. "I love you so much. I hate to see you upset. I don't think I'll go to Lewistown quite yet."

Her mother pulled back. "Oh, *jah*, you're going. I'll be just fine. I'm just having a little pity party. By tonight, I'll be my old self again. Now you go write that letter and I'll sweep up the hair that fell."

"Mamm…"

"No *Mamm*! You do as I say, young lady. I'm still your *mudder*, and you have to listen."

Martha smiled and gave her a final hug before going into her room and writing the note to Deborah. She was so proud of her mother for being the way she was. Long, beautiful tresses or bald mattered not at all. She was the most wonderful mother in the world.

Jeremiah seemed like his old self once more. He whistled quite often as he worked and talked to Paul just like he used to. Paul was relieved and put any thought of talking to him about what happened between him and Hazel totally out of his mind. It was just a mistake. A moment of weakness. It sure wouldn't happen again. It troubled him though, that sometimes at night he'd dream of Hazel. Once he pictured her in his arms, her belly swollen with child. When he awoke from that dream, he was drenched in perspiration. He had gotten up and gone over to the workshop to work on one of their projects. Sleep was out of the question. He'd even prayed about it and asked God to take any lustful thoughts away from him. It seemed to help, but the memory of that dream continued to haunt him.

One afternoon, while Paul was working, Ebenezer stopped by on his way to the hardware store to pick up supplies.

"Well, nice to see my old friend gets out once in a while," Paul teased. "What brings you here?"

"Deborah asked me to stop by to tell you she got a letter from Martha yesterday. She's planning to visit us next week. She thought you should know so you can make plans ahead."

"Great! She didn't write to me about it."

"She probably wanted to check with us first. Anyway, Deb wrote back today and stuck it in the mailbox to tell her it was fine. She plans to come next Thursday and stay two nights. Hope you'll have your meals with us."

"*Danki*. Probably not all of them, but Deborah's a *gut* cook and we wouldn't want to hurt her feelings," he added, grinning over at his friend.

They chatted a few more minutes, and after Ebenezer left, Jeremiah looked over and smiled. "I heard. Sorry, I wasn't trying to listen in."

"No problem. I'd have to talk to you about it anyway."

"I guess you're pretty excited."

"Oh *jah*, for sure! We don't get to talk much on the phone anymore, so we need to see each other in person."

"Or things might fade?" Jeremiah asked, raising his brows.

"That won't happen, but it is hard to be apart. I'm

glad things are working out for you and Hazel, Jeremiah. She's a nice *maed*."

"I know." He set the wood he was sanding aside and stood back, folding his arms. "I was pretty worried for a while that she would never get over you, but I think now, she is."

"I'm sure she is."

"So, you ever think you made a mistake by leaving her?"

"No, it was the right thing to do."

"I'm relieved. Anyway, our workload should be down by the end of next week, so take as much time off as you want. I might even take one of those days off. All work and no play... Why don't we go somewhere together? All four of us? Maybe there's a fair somewhere nearby. Or we can eat at a buffet."

"Sure. Why not?" Paul said, smiling over. Personally, the idea terrified him, but he certainly couldn't let on. "You can check it out and talk it over with Hazel. I'm sure Martha will be fine with whatever we decide."

"*Jah*, she and Hazel are pretty *gut* friends. Okay, I'll mark the calendar. I'll even give Ben the day off. He's a hard worker and could use a break as well."

"It's *gut* he has a truck and can drive. He should be back soon with the rest of the cherry wood." Paul felt safer talking about wood. He wondered why he hadn't gotten a letter from Martha when his phone rang. Lo and behold, it was her!

"Hi, Paul. It's me. I have only a minute before I have to take my *dawdi* to the doctor's, but I wanted to tell you I'm coming to Lewistown, if it works out with Deborah."

"I know all about it! Eb just stopped by to tell me and it's fine with them for the dates you mentioned."

"Oh, I'm so glad. I can't wait to see you again."

"Your *mamm* must be doing pretty *gut* for you to be able to get away."

"She insisted I take time off. Bless her, she's doing better though with the nausea. They gave her stronger medicine."

"I'm real glad, Martha. Please give your folks my best. Your *grossmammi* and *dawdi*, too."

"I will. I'll try to get going early on Thursday so we can spend most of the day together. You will be able to take off work then?"

"*Jah*, it's all taken care of. We're even closing the shop on Friday."

"That's wonderful-*gut*! I have to go now, Paul. I'll see you Thursday and you can tell me everything that's going on."

After they hung up, he grinned over at Jeremiah, who hadn't missed a word. "How's that for timing?"

Jeremiah chuckled. "Pretty cool. I hear the truck. Let's go give Ben a hand."

He patted Paul on the back as he walked past him towards the back door. Paul reached for his straw hat. That June sun was strong. Time was moving so quickly, maybe waiting till the following fall to marry wouldn't seem like forever, after all.

Chapter Seventeen

Daniel wiped his forehead with an old cloth he'd brought with him. That sun was getting to him. He probably should have arrived earlier to paint the English family's clapboard home. This was the second day and he figured it would take him more than a week to complete the job. He hadn't met the husband yet, but he had been introduced to their twelve-year-old son and their college-age daughter, Brianna. What a knockout. She had been wearing skimpy denim shorts with a clinging knit shirt which revealed her lovely schoolgirl figure. It had been difficult to keep his eyes off the young woman. He wondered where she was today. Of course, it was only ten-thirty. English teenagers liked to sleep in late, he'd discovered. Amish teens were not able to indulge in that luxury, since they had their chores lined up for them—summer or winter.

He drank the rest of the jug of water he'd brought with him and heard the front door open and close. When he looked over, Brianna was standing, hands on hips, watching him.

"Hot?"

"*Jah*, very."

"You should take a break."

"I just might. Would you mind filling my bottle with water when you have a chance?" he asked, noting her attire today was every bit as revealing as yesterday's. It took all his strength to keep his gaze on her eyes, which were exquisitely framed with some kind of blue stuff, which highlighted the blue of her eyes and her dark, curved lashes.

"I can do it now." She reached over and he handed her his empty bottle. A flowery scent reached his nostrils and he knew he was beginning to blush. Hopefully, she wouldn't notice.

When she returned, he was doing the final strokes on the section he'd started earlier. He wiped his hands and took the bottle from her. "*Danki*, or I should say thank you."

She smiled broadly. "It's cute to hear you talk. Don't change on my account. I have Amish friends. I understand some of the stuff they say in the Deutsch. So, you paint for a living?"

"And farm. This just brings in some extra money."

"Do you drive?"

"Horses," he answered, grinning.

She pointed to the open garage at the side of the house. "That green Chevy is mine, if you ever want to try driving. My parents bought it for my high school graduation last year."

"Are you working?"

"No way! I go to Temple University in Philadelphia and I need a break."

"Sure, I've heard of it. *Gut* school?"

"I guess. I wouldn't be going, but my parents insisted."

"What are you studying?" he asked after taking a long swig of water.

"General stuff. I'm not sure what I want to do. Maybe I'll be a nurse or something. They make a lot of money."

"That's hard work, isn't it?"

"I guess so. Maybe I'll win the lottery and won't have to work."

"I wouldn't count on it," he said, smiling over. "So, you have a boyfriend?"

"I did, but he got boring. I broke off a couple months ago. I'm dating a couple guys now, but nothing serious. I have too much I want to do in life to worry about keeping a guy happy."

"I bet you get a lot of guys asking you out."

"Why do you say that?" she asked, flirting with her eyes.

"Well, you know. You're quite a looker."

She giggled. "*Danki!* You're not so bad yourself."

"I bet you've never dated an Amishman."

"Nope. Are they different?"

"Why don't you go out with me tonight and find out for yourself?"

"You're tempting me."

He grinned and poured the water that was left over his hair to cool off. "You can drive and maybe teach me how. We can go out to eat, if you want."

"Better than that, I know a place where they have a great DJ and a dance floor. Are you up for it?"

He nodded. "For sure, though I'm not that great a dancer."

"I can teach you. I can teach you lots of things."

He wondered how much experience this young woman may have had. This could be an interesting night. He'd planned to stop off at Martha's on his way home, but a cool shower and fresh English clothing, which fortunately he'd kept, would take the place of that visit.

They settled on a time and she disappeared into her home. Her brother came out once and hung around for a while. His name was Dave, but he apparently got bored and went off to find a friend. Daniel decided to call it a day around two, and went home to clean up. These English girls knew how to have a good time. He should have kept his apartment.

Martha baked several loaves of bread the morning she left for Lewistown. She'd baked off brownies and chocolate chip cookies the night before, mainly for her father. She'd even found a recipe for sugarless cookies, which she made specifically for her grandfather, and she dropped them off at the *dawdi haus*, just before the driver arrived.

Her mother was quieter than usual as she waited outside with Martha for her ride. "Now, you be sure to get enough sleep. You shouldn't be alone with Paul either. Why don't you see him at Deborah's house? Maybe you could watch their children and give them a break as well."

"We'll see, *Mamm*. I'm going for a *break*, not to spend my whole time babysitting!"

"Well, you needn't get sharp with me."

"I didn't mean to. It came out wrong."

"It sure did. I'm sorry if I've been such a burden—"

"*Mamm*, stop! Let's not argue. I don't want to go off with you mad at me."

"I'm not mad, just a little disappointed that you'd talk to me that way."

Martha let out a long sigh. "Here comes my ride. I'll see you Saturday some time."

"By noon? So, you can help with the dinner?"

"I don't know, *Mamm*. Please don't pressure me."

"I never do that. I encouraged you to take this break. I know it must be hard to take care of a sick person all day, every day."

"I don't look at it that way. Oh, *Mamm*, he's parking. I really have to go. Say good-bye to *Daed* for me. He's too far out in the field for him to hear me." Martha leaned over and kissed her mother's *kapp*. She ignored the trembling lips, and climbed in next to Hank, one of their drivers. For some reason, her mother's attitude annoyed her. She managed to wave, and her mother gave a weak wave in return.

Once on the road, she and Hank conversed, which helped get her mind off her departure. He was about her father's age and she enjoyed talking with him. She got caught up on news, though it seemed almost like fiction to hear about all the turmoil swirling around the world, while she lived a relatively quiet life. Another reason she loved being Amish. Her world seemed remote from the rest of civilization.

Paul came out of the workshop as the car pulled in. This time, without fear of parents watching, he took her in his arms immediately, though he did not prolong their embrace and avoided even a simple kiss on the cheek.

He wouldn't embarrass Martha by showing that much affection in front of the driver.

After paying Hank, which Paul insisted on doing, he removed her small suitcase from the back seat, and they headed for the shop. Jeremiah greeted her enthusiastically, while Paul put his tools away. He and Martha went back to the home they hoped to live in eventually. Her heart swelled as she walked into the sweet living room and discovered Paul had added a red sofa, which sat across from their fireplace. Wildflowers, set in a glass milk bottle, had been placed on one of the windowsills.

He grinned as he walked over to the flowers, taking her by the hand. "Like them?"

"They're lovely, Paul. You're so thoughtful."

"Actually, my *mudder* suggested it. She wants us to go over sometime while you're here."

"I'd love to. I'll thank *her* for the flowers then," she added, smiling over.

"Oh, it was her idea, but I'm the one who picked them," he said.

"Then this is for you." She placed her arms around his neck and drew his head down to hers for a real kiss. At that moment, he knew where his heart lay. Whatever happened with Hazel that awful night was fleshly passion. What he had with his Martha was beautiful and real love. He would be faithful to her for life, of that he was sure.

They spent the day taking walks and weeding his small vegetable garden behind their home-to-be. She was impressed that he found the time, though he'd only planted tomatoes and zucchini. After clearing out the majority of weeds, they stood back and admired their work.

"When we marry, Paul, I'll have you extend the garden and I'll add all kinds of vegetables. I love to garden and I know how to can and make pickles and lots of things wives need to know."

"Sweetheart, if we end up buying everything we eat, I won't mind, as long as we're together." He put his arm around her waist. "You've lost weight, haven't you?"

"A little, I guess."

"Are you working too hard?"

"*Nee.* I think I just eat less when I'm worried about things."

"Your *mudder*?" he asked.

"And you. It's not *gut* to be apart this much. What if you find someone else?"

"Or you, Martha. I know there must be a dozen guys interested in you. How do you keep them all away?"

"Oh, I have a whip! They're not allowed to be too close."

He grinned. "Do you have to use it on that Daniel guy?"

"Oh, for sure! He's the worst."

"Seriously, does he still come around, pretending to be so concerned for your *mudder*?"

"Not as much. I discourage him anytime I see him. He just won't give up, though. It's pretty annoying, actually. I told him at lunch the other—"

"Honey, why was he at your place for lunch?"

"Oh dear, you're going to take this all wrong. Paul, you have nothing to worry about, I promise you, but we are friends. He behaves okay now, usually, but he did take me out once. It ended in a disaster. I don't know why I accepted. I guess I was just so tired of being home all the time and we had seen each other at market. I paid for my own meal. Please don't be mad at me."

"I'm not angry. I just wish you wouldn't even have him as a friend. You have enough women friends, don't you?"

"That's not the point. You need to trust me, Paul."

"Honey, I do trust you, but I don't trust that guy. He might even get rough with you. Remember how he acted?"

"I don't get that close to him anymore. I don't fully trust him, either."

"Well, I won't say anymore, but you know how I feel."

"What should we do tomorrow? I'm so excited—we have a whole day, just you and me."

He suddenly looked chagrined. "Uh, oh. I agreed we'd spend most of the day with Jeremiah and Hazel."

"You didn't!"

"I'm afraid I did. I guess I wasn't thinking. Maybe we can get out of it."

"Never mind. It might be fun. I haven't seen Hazel for ages. I'm glad it's going so *gut* for them."

"Umm."

"Did they tell you when they plan to marry?"

"Not yet. I don't ask."

"I'm sure Hazel will tell me when we see each other. I have to spend time with Deborah, too. Maybe we can give her and Eb a couple hours to themselves."

"You mean babysit five *kinner*?" Paul's face blanched.

"Paul, we may have a dozen *kinner* someday. May as well get some practice now."

"Phew! I guess you're right. Don't get me wrong—

I love kids, but right now it's you I want to be with. I wish I'd told Jeremiah it wouldn't work out."

"It's too late. We don't want to hurt his feelings. Besides, I should get to know your business partner better."

"It sounds like you've accepted the idea of moving here. Am I reading you right?"

"I want to say yes, but I can't yet. I try not to think about it, Paul, at least until we get a report on my mother's cancer. She won't be getting an MRI until the chemo is done. I'm so afraid it won't be enough treatment."

"You have to be optimistic, Martha. They can cure real hard cases today."

"*Jah*, I know. But since she had cancer before…"

"Well, we have to just wait for the report, I guess."

"And pray."

"*Jah*, I've been praying for her every day, as well."

"*Danki*. So, what do you and Jeremiah have planned?"

"I told him to do the planning and we'll go along with it."

"I hope we'll spend some time outdoors. It's been a beautiful month so far. Not too hot."

"*Jah*. I've been working weekends with my *daed*, when I have a chance. Got all the fields planted. Of course, my *bruders* helped as well. I think you'll learn to love my family, Martha. We're very close."

"So far, I like them all. Your nieces and nephews are adorable. When are we going over to visit with them?"

"*Mamm* suggested breakfast tomorrow."

"That would be fun. My favorite meal."

"She promised to make her Swedish oatmeal pancakes, if we go there."

"Yum! I hope she'll share her recipe."

"Oh, *jah*, I'll make sure she does."

"I think I'm getting a little better at cooking, Paul."

"Please don't worry about your cooking, honey. I can eat anything."

"Yipes, that sounds bad. I'm not that awful!" She grinned over. "Maybe I'll get Hazel's recipe for honey wheat bread. She brought some over to Deborah's once, and it was delicious."

"We should probably go over to Deb and Eb's place soon. The *buwe* are all excited to see you."

"I bet the twins are getting big."

"*Jah*, they're pretty cute."

"I can't believe she'll be having another one soon. With *Mamm* needing me, I won't be able to help out, I'm afraid."

"It's okay. Eb has gotten so much better with the *kinner*, I'm sure between him and her *schwesters*, she'll be fine."

"You do want a big family, don't you, Paul?"

"Of course. As many as the *gut* Lord provides."

Martha wished she could cook their dinner in the home they'd share one day, but the pantry was nearly empty and Paul seemed to have the meals all worked out. After putting the gardening tools away and washing up, they made their way over to Deb and Eb's place where they were greeted enthusiastically by everyone. Even the babies seemed excited, though she was sure they didn't really remember her at their young age.

The men took the boys outside to play, after they settled down somewhat. Martha helped Deborah prepare their supper, while the twins played together in a playpen set up at the end of the kitchen. Deborah had made her wonderful German potato salad and she sliced up a ham, which came from their own farm. Simple and delicious.

"I heard you and Paul are going to spend tomorrow with my *schwester* and Jeremiah."

"*Jah*, truthfully, I would have preferred just spending the day alone with Paul, but he'd already made plans."

"Mmm. Too bad."

"Oh, we want to come back then and let you and Eb take a couple hours off for yourselves and we'll watch the *kinner*."

"Oh, how sweet! *Danki*. We might just take advantage of that. We could take a buggy ride, maybe."

"We'll come back here to sit for you before the sun sets so you can drive safely."

"And Paul told us a couple days ago that his folks want you there for breakfast tomorrow."

"*Jah*, we're going to be busy every minute, which would please my *mudder*." She told Deborah about their little tiff before she left and her mother's fears about her being alone with Paul.

Deborah listened and nodded as she spoke. "Come sit. We have a half hour before supper." They sat across from each other at the long kitchen table. "Maybe it's none of my business, Martha, but maybe your *mamm* is expecting too much from you. I mean, you need to think of yourself once in a while."

"Oh, she actually suggested I take some time off. You don't understand, right now while she's so sick, she really needs me."

"I know she does, but Paul said you want him to move to Lancaster when you marry. He has his business now, Martha. And a wonderful-*gut* home for you to live in. It's not like you'd be a million miles apart. You could see your family often."

"People really don't understand. I was adopted. They didn't have to raise me, but they did, and they love me like their own."

"I agree, but all parents have to eventually let go of their children and let them live their own lives."

"Paul and I haven't really decided about where we'll live yet. I want to see how she is before I decide. If she's still sick…"

"Well, I shouldn't say anything, but I think Hazel still has eyes for Paul."

"She's going to marry Jeremiah!" Martha said shocked.

"Maybe."

"But Paul broke up with her ages ago. He doesn't even see her, does he?" She looked over at Deb trying to read her face. She had a strained expression. "Deb, have they been seeing each other? Tell me the truth."

"I've said too much already. You'll have to ask him."

"That sounds like a yes."

"Don't, Martha. I'm sure there's nothing to worry about with Paul. I just wanted to warn you that Paul could be vulnerable. I'm glad you came and I think you should get together with him more frequently. Guys get lonely."

Martha pulled on her *kapp* strings and stared into space. "There's more I should know. I can read between your words, Deborah."

"I wish I'd kept my big mouth shut," she said. "Just talk it over with Paul and make plans to see each other more often. He said you don't even talk on the phone that much."

"Maybe I'll charge up my phone he gave me. At least, we can talk every day that way. I guess I just expect too much from him, though for pity's sake—my *mudder* is a sick woman! You'd think he'd try a little harder to understand."

"He's a *gut* man, Martha. Don't forget that, but he's still a man—Amish or not."

"I'm not sure what you're trying to tell me. I guess we'll have a talk, maybe while we watch the kids. Once they're down for the night, that is."

"If we get back too soon, we'll make something up so we can leave you alone together."

"*Jah. Gut* idea. Just don't tell my *mudder*," Martha said, with a forced smile.

Chapter Eighteen

"You've been awfully quiet this evening," Paul remarked as he sat alone with Martha while Deb and Eb put the children down for the night. "Is anything wrong?"

"*Nee*, just tired, I guess. I'm almost ready to go to bed though. I was up real early this morning."

"I guess I'll get ready to leave then," he said, his eyes cast down.

She knew she'd hurt him, but Deb's words kept running through her mind. She needed time to process what she'd heard. Hazel, of all people. She thought she was such a good friend.

"I'll pick you up around nine for breakfast, okay?"

"Sure, that's fine. I'm looking forward to seeing your family again." She made every effort to sound normal and pleasant.

"*Jah.*"

His sad eyes made it apparent that her efforts had failed. "Paul, we'll have a nice day together, no matter what we do or who we're with. I'm just tired tonight. Forgive me if I seem down."

"You were so different before. Was it something Deb said?"

"Would she have something to tell me that would upset me?"

His eyes met hers and they were silent for a moment, but not before she read trouble by his serious expression.

"I may as well tell you," Martha said haltingly. "She let it slip that you and Hazel have seen each other— alone. Was there more you want to tell me?"

"I don't know why she'd mention it. It really was nothing. Sometimes, just like you and Daniel, things happen and you find yourself alone with someone you'd prefer not to be with. It happens to everyone."

"She thinks Hazel still has eyes for you."

"She's wrong!" he said too emphatically. "We're friends. That's it."

"Don't get so upset. I'll take your word for it."

"I guess I'm just annoyed that she'd give you that impression."

"Maybe because she's Hazel's sister and they talk about things."

"Well, you'll see tomorrow. There's absolutely nothing between us. Nothing!"

"You're overreacting, Paul. I don't like it." She felt her heart palpitate overtime. There was more here, of that she was certain.

"I hear Eb coming down. We can talk tomorrow," he said softly, a total change from his angry expression the moment before.

So, whom was he angry with? Her? Deborah?

"Well, I think they're going to behave now," Eb said,

referring to his children. He looked from Paul, over to Martha. "You guys okay?"

"We're fine. Martha's tired, is all. I'm gonna leave now."

"It's only half past seven," Eb said.

"It's been a long day for me, Eb," Martha said, attempting to smile naturally. "Tomorrow will be another long day."

"Sure. I understand. Don't you want to wait for Deborah to come down?" he asked Paul, who was reaching for his straw hat.

"I'll see her tomorrow. Just say *gut nacht* for me," Paul said as he nodded over to Martha and left.

"Huh. Paul don't seem like himself tonight," Eb said. "You guys fighting?"

"We don't fight."

"Arguing then?"

"It's okay, Eb. Just a little misunderstanding."

"Sorry to hear that. He's sure been missing you a lot. I'm surprised, is all."

"We'll get it all straightened out tomorrow."

"Deb said you and her *schwester* and Jeremiah are going on a hike. *Jah?*"

"I guess so. I'm just here to follow orders."

"Hmm. You don't sound too happy."

"I'll go up and see if Deborah needs help. I may read for a while then. I'll stay upstairs in the room you set up for me."

"It's pretty small, I'm afraid. It was just a big closet before we put a cot in there. Lucky, it has a small window. At least it's more private than the sofa was when you were here before."

"It's fine. See you tomorrow, Eb."

* * *

He nodded and then sat on the sofa and picked up a farming magazine he'd bought. Paul was his best friend, but sometimes he couldn't figure him out to save the world. Glad all that courting was done and over with between him and Deborah. They got along just fine, even with all the *kinner* to tend to.

Lizzy sat waiting for her sister to complete the chemo treatment. She was glad her brother-in-law wasn't along today. She never did cotton up to him. She set a magazine aside as she saw Sarah coming down the hallway on the arm of the nurse. She looked so pale. Poor *maed*.

Once the next appointment was confirmed, Lizzy took Sarah's arm and led her out to the waiting buggy. "You okay?"

"Oh, *jah*. As *gut* as can be expected. This is the last chemo for a while. I get three whole weeks off now, before they start up again."

"Why do they do that?"

"I guess to let my body repair itself a little. That chemo is real strong, you know. It's in my body trying to destroy the bad cells, but I guess some of the *gut* ones get hurt as well."

"I guess. These are sure *schmaert* doctors they have here."

"Everyone is real nice to me, Lizzy. Sometimes, better than my own family."

Lizzy helped her sister into the buggy and then went around and climbed in the driver's side. Before starting their journey home, she turned to Sarah. "Now that's a funny thing to say. We've all tried to be as helpful as we can."

"You've been *gut*, Lizzy. I didn't mean you."

"Well, who did you mean?"

"It's mainly Martha."

"You've got to be kidding! That young lady has been doing everything possible to help you. Shame on you for even saying such a thing."

Sarah looked over. "But she's doing it because she thinks she has to. She couldn't wait to leave this morning."

"Well, my dear, she does miss Paul you know. Of course, she's in a hurry to get to see him. You're just lucky she's here at all, for heaven's sake. Be grateful for her devotion to you."

"She got very testy with me this morning. It sure hurt my feelings. I don't want her here because she feels she has to be."

"Oh, I can't even talk to you. You don't make any sense. Martha is here because she loves you. She wants to help you in every way. My goodness, the girl just needs to see her future husband once in a while. It's only natural. I've been thinking about things and maybe we all expect too much from her. She should be living her own life."

"She does."

"*Jah?* She had her own apartment and job, a future with a *gut* Amishman, and she gave all that up to come be with you. At the time, I thought it was a *gut* idea, but I'm here for you. You have a husband who cares, and it's not like you can't get around and even cook."

Sarah burst into tears. She covered her face with her hands. "You have no idea how hard this is. I may be dying."

Lizzy held the reins in one hand and reached across

to pat her sister's knee. "I'm sorry, Sarah. You're right. I don't know what you're dealing with really. Forgive me. Just be kinder to Martha in your thoughts. She's a wonderful-*gut* girl and does so much for you, you just have to keep that in your mind."

"Oh, Lizzy, what if she marries him and moves away? I don't think I could stand it."

"So, move there, too. Your land is worth a lot of money. You could afford it."

"Then I'd be leaving you."

"I'm a grown woman, *schwester*. And we wouldn't be that far apart. I'd visit you and you'd visit me. Goodness! We'd survive just fine."

"I don't know. I never considered moving. My husband isn't ready to give up farming. He's still strong, and we have my folks."

"Well, you could wait a couple of years to make the move."

"You think I'm being selfish, *jah*?"

"I didn't say that."

"But you're thinking it. I know that. Maybe I am. I want to do what *Gott* would have me do. I'll pray about all this. You're right. I was too rough on Martha this morning. Now I feel bad. Maybe I'll let her use her cell phone. I don't have to mention it to anyone else, though I'll need to get Melvin to agree. That way she can talk to Paul every day. That should help."

"That's a *gut* decision. I like it. Tell her as soon as you get Melvin's okay."

"I'm not going to mention your idea about our moving there. Not yet, anyway. That will take much more thought and prayer."

"I agree. I just wanted to mention it as a possibility."

"*Danki*. You're a *gut schwester*. Wonderful, really."

Her words to Martha earlier in the day rang through her mind as they made their way home. It had been wrong of her to talk to her daughter that way. She would be a better *mudder* from now on—that was for sure.

Chapter Nineteen

Every day, Rose checked her mailbox in the hopes of finding a letter from Lancaster. All she received were the normal ads and impersonal mail from her business accounts. This morning she sat ripping up the unnecessary mail as she sipped her second cup of coffee.

Why would her daughter write? She was a complete stranger. Perhaps, she hated her for leaving her with others to raise. What did she expect after all these years of absence? Or perhaps, she hadn't been back to the ice cream shop. Yes, that was it. She didn't even have the letter in her possession yet. When she did, she'd…what? Destroy it? Write back immediately? Call? Oh, if only she'd do something! The waiting was horrid. Enough!

It was time to lay that hope aside and continue with her normal life. She had a good life, after all. Enough friends to avoid total loneliness and fortunately she was comfortable in her home and made a nice living with her writing. She might even accept a dinner date with the new neighbor, if he asked. He'd seemed interested in talking with her when she took a casserole over to him on his moving day. At the time, she thought he was married, but it turned out the woman she saw helping him was his younger sister. Of course, if he didn't turn out to be interested, that would be fine, too.

Rose finished her coffee, washed out her mug and returned to her computer to immerse herself in her latest manuscript. Her daughter, Martha, was once more pushed to the back of her mind—though never eliminated from her thoughts and dreams.

Paul arrived a few minutes early at Eb and Deb's house to pick up Martha for their breakfast at his parents' home. Martha was feeding cereal to the twins while Deborah fried up sausage for the rest of the family.

Martha looked up and smiled at Paul. She looked more like herself. Perhaps she was just tired the night before and they could avoid any talk of the past. He sat next to Martha and took one of the small spoons from the bowl and helped with the girls' breakfast.

"Danki," Martha said with a nod. "It will go quicker with two of us feeding them. Aren't they adorable, Paul?"

"Oh *jah*."

Deborah looked over and smiled. "That will be you two one of these days," she said grinning.

"It would be fun to have twins," Paul said, glancing over at Martha to see her response.

"I sure would need help," Martha said. "I saw what it was like when these little ones were born. I don't think Deb got more than three hours sleep at a time, did you?" she asked, looking over at her friend.

"I was lucky to sleep that long," she said with a smile. "*Jah*, it was hard at first. I sure needed you there to help,

Martha. I'll never forget how much you did for me. *Gott* brought you here for a purpose, for sure."

"I thought He did that for me," Paul said with a crooked smile. "He wanted us to meet."

"Maybe He had two reasons then," Martha said, though at the moment she wondered if Paul had really been part of God's plan for her life. It sure had complicated her life in many ways, though her heart still belonged to the handsome young Amishman—if he wanted it.

The twins finished up and after wiping their faces, Martha and Paul placed them in the playpen, while Deborah called the boys in for their breakfast. After saying good-bye, Martha and Paul made their way out to his buggy and they started over for his parents' home.

"Did you sleep okay?" he asked.

"Not real great, but I'm all right," she said.

"It sure is a nice day for a hike. I see you have *gut* sneakers on."

"*Jah*, I wear sneakers a lot. They're comfortable."

"*Jah.*"

"How long is the hike going to take?"

"I don't really know. Jeremiah has it mapped out. We can ask him when we meet up."

"And what time is that going to be?" she asked, frowning.

"He said to meet him at the shop by noon. Hazel is bringing lunch and we can eat it there or take it with us."

"So, they're really running the whole show."

"Martha, they planned it so we could have a fun day together, not to be bossy."

"I'm sure."

"Look, if you don't want to go, I'll call it off."

"Don't be silly. It's too late for that. I'm sure Hazel has prepared a banquet by now and we mustn't hurt her feelings."

"Wow, you sure sound mad. I've never seen you like this."

"Goodness, I'm not mad!" she said, obviously angry at the whole idea.

"Well, I hope you'll calm down in front of my parents."

"I'll be fine!" She folded her arms and glared out the window as the horse trotted along the road. They didn't speak until he reached his parents' drive.

"Are you calmed down yet?" he asked, looking over for the first time since the tiff.

"*Jah*. I'm sorry. I shouldn't have talked like that. I'll be okay now."

"I hope so," he said as he brought the horse to a stop and got out. Instead of helping her out, he headed straight for the back door. She climbed down and tried to catch up. They got to the doorway about the same time. When they entered, his mother came right over and gave her a hug.

"*Wilkum*," she said to Martha as Paul's father came in to join them.

"*Danki*," Martha said, managing a smile, though she was miserable inside.

"I hope you like Swedish oatmeal pancakes," his mother was saying.

Martha nodded. "Oh *jah*, for sure. I've been dreaming about them." She glanced over at Paul, who looked pleased at her response.

"You and Paul sit down and I'll bring out the fruit I cut up. We can sit and eat that first."

So, the breakfast began and all feelings were set aside—temporarily. There was pleasant conversation and Martha responded to their friendly overtures with her normal sweet personality. The friction from earlier dissipated and for a while she and Paul relaxed and enjoyed each other's company. She said a silent prayer that it would last.

After the meal was finished, Martha dried the dishes for his mother and Paul went out to the barn with his father to help with the chores. They saw little of each other until noon, when Paul came in and mentioned they needed to leave.

Once in the buggy, Martha reached over for Paul's hand as they discussed the breakfast that had just taken place. He reciprocated and showed his pleasure in her small gesture. He held her hand tightly until he had to release it to bring his horse to a stop at their shop.

"I see Hazel is already here," he commented as he went around to help Martha down.

"I sure can't eat yet. Those pancakes filled me up real *gut*," Martha said as they headed over to the entrance.

When they went through the doors, Hazel and Jeremiah were standing in the showroom talking. They came right over and Hazel embraced Martha enthusiastically. Martha made a weak effort to respond, but it was obvious there was tension, though Hazel seemed to ignore it—if she even realized her friend's lack of fervor was directed at her.

Jeremiah shook Martha's hand.

Hazel then went over to Paul, who reached out with his hand for a handshake. "Goodness, we're better friends than that, Paul. Give me a hug," she said, appearing innocent of anything more. His body stiffened as he held her at a distance. Martha watched carefully, unhappy with Hazel's forwardness. It was not normal for an Amish woman to act so bold.

"I hope you're hungry," Hazel added, moving back to Jeremiah's side. "I spent all morning frying chicken and making salads."

"We just had a huge breakfast at my parents' place," Paul said. "I hope we can wait awhile."

"Oh, sure. That's fine. Maybe we should take a buggy ride then—until you get hungry. The hike would take too long, wouldn't it, Jeremiah?" Hazel asked.

"*Jah*, I figure two hours, up and back," he said.

"A buggy ride sounds *gut*," Paul said. "Don't you think so, Martha?"

"Whatever you decide. I'm just here for the ride."

Hazel laughed. "Then ride, we will! Do you want to take my buggy? It's all hitched up."

"So is mine," Paul said. "Let's use that one."

Martha was disappointed at the suggestion. That would mean he'd be driving, and she had hoped they could sit together in the back and maybe get past their disturbing start. He might even be able to sneak in a kiss, but this way...

"Better idea," Hazel said. "Take my buggy and the guys can ride in the front while Martha and I catch up on our girl-talk."

"*Gut* idea," Jeremiah said. "I have to talk to Paul about a new job we just got. I heard today the Wilsons are going to accept our terms on their new library shelving, partner."

Martha looked over at Paul, who shrugged. He didn't look terribly upset about the seating arrangement, so who was she to be concerned?

After they pulled out of the drive, Hazel started asking Martha about her mother's condition. "It's sure important for you to be there with her through all of this," she said, appearing to show genuine concern. "She could never handle it by herself."

"She has my *daed* and her *schwester* and their whole family," Martha reminded her.

"Oh, *jah*, but it's your *dochder* you need the most."

"I'm glad I can be there. I just miss Paul."

"I'm sure he misses you, too, when he has time to think about it. He and Jeremiah have been working terrible long hours sometimes."

"I heard."

"I'm taking their meals over again."

"I didn't know."

"*Jah*, I feel bad for them, so I just cook a little extra every day. I think they appreciate it."

"I'm sure."

"Especially Paul. He loves my soups—even more than Jeremiah. I promised I'd give you some of my recipes if you two end up together someday."

"That's nice."

"*Jah*, we'll be neighbors if Jeremiah and I get married."

"Do you think you will marry?"

Hazel tilted her head. "Maybe."

Martha leaned over to whisper. "Has he asked you yet?"

"Kind of. We were having some problems for a while, so we're just now dating again."

"I didn't know that."

"I'm surprised Paul didn't tell you. He was so helpful when I needed a shoulder to cry on."

"Oh."

"*Jah*, he's very understanding. Of course, I've known that about him for a long time. Don't forget, we were real serious at one time."

"No, I haven't forgotten."

"Of course, now we're just *gut* friends, but I can tell him anything."

"Hmm."

"And he talks to me about personal things, too. Like you thinking about wanting to stay in Lancaster County."

"We've talked about it."

"I don't think that went over too well with Paul. In fact, I know it didn't. He's got a *gut* business going, Martha. You'd be asking a lot. Maybe too much."

"That's for us to decide, Hazel. It's really none of your business."

"I guess I spoke out of turn. It's just that he got it off his chest one time, and I was the one to hear about it. I think it helped for him to unload. A guy has to open up sometimes. He was always able to share his deepest thoughts with me. But I'm sure he does the same with you."

"*Jah*, of course." Martha's stomach did a flip. It was so obvious that Hazel still had feelings for Paul. How much of what she was saying was true, and how much was she inflating their close friendship?

Paul looked back at the girls. "You two must have a lot to catch up on," he said, with a smile.

"Oh, we do, Paul," Hazel said, smiling sweetly. "*Danki*, for giving us this chance."

"We can stop at the town park, if you want, so we can walk around a little before heading back to eat."

"We'd better go back soon. I made strawberry pie for dessert. I know that's your favorite, Paul."

"It's Jeremiah's favorite, too, isn't it?" he asked.

"I'm not sure. Ask him," she said, as she turned back towards Martha. "Paul asks me to bake it almost every week. I think I've spoiled him a little. I sure hope you like to bake, Martha. He loves his sweets."

"I know."

When they got out to walk around, Martha went right over to Paul and took ahold of his hand. His brows rose, but he looked pleased as he squeezed her hand. "I've missed you," he whispered in her ear as they walked behind the other couple.

"I hope that's true."

"Honey, you know it's true."

"I guess so. It's just…well, we can talk later. I just have to get through this afternoon."

He looked intently into her eyes, nearly tripping on the pavement. "I can see you're upset. It's because we're not alone, isn't it? I really goofed by accepting Jeremiah's suggestion. I'm real sorry, Martha. It just kind of happened."

"It's okay. Tonight we'll be alone. Sort of. Once the kids are in bed."

"I can't wait. What time is your ride coming tomorrow?"

"In the morning around ten. I tried to make it later, but it's the only time he could come get me."

"We'll have to make the most of this evening then."

She nodded as Hazel turned around and pointed out a bench under an oak tree. "There's our favorite bench, Paul. Remember?"

"Actually, no," he said, his face turning scarlet.

Hazel giggled. "That's where you gave me my first kiss."

Jeremiah rolled his eyes. "Nice."

"I'd forgotten," Paul said quickly.

"I don't think so," she said in a sing-songy voice. "He's a *gut* kisser, *jah*?" she called over to Martha.

"Goodness, Hazel," Martha said angrily. "You sure don't sound like an Amish *maed*! We don't talk about things like that, for heaven's sake."

Hazel continued to laugh as she grabbed for Jeremiah's hand and lifted her face for a kiss from her newer boyfriend. Jeremiah laughed hesitantly and gave her a quick peck, obviously embarrassed by her brazenness.

After a walk around the edge of the small park, they headed back to the buggy, only this time Paul insisted on sitting in the back with Martha.

Halfway home, he leaned over and kissed Martha lightly on the lips. "I love you," he whispered.

"I sure hope so," she answered and she swallowed hard to keep tears from forming.

The food Hazel had prepared was delicious, though Martha made no comment. She was fuming from their conversation and couldn't bring herself to be hypocritical and shower praises on this woman who was so obviously still in love with Paul. Why didn't Jeremiah see it? Poor guy.

The hike took place and Paul held Martha's hand the entire time and avoided any jibes coming from Hazel. What a mistake to spend a whole afternoon with them.

Finally, the ordeal was over. They headed back to Eb and Deborah's house, just in time for the boys to be bathed. Martha gave Deborah a hand while Paul and Eb sat in the kitchen, each feeding a twin their cereal for the night. For a while, Hazel was not on the forefront of her mind. For a little while, she could enjoy being with a real friend. A married friend.

Chapter Twenty

Deborah made sure the boys understood they had to obey Paul and Martha. They fretted when they learned their parents were going out for the evening, but they agreed not to cause a fuss when it was their bedtime.

Martha read *The Three Little Pigs* to them from one of their Golden Books. Paul listened as he sat on the edge of one of their beds. He added a few remarks and made animal noises at the appropriate times, which caused the boys to giggle merrily. Eventually, Martha turned down the kerosene lantern and they used it to make their way down the darkening staircase. They sat together on the sofa, Paul resting his arm around her shoulder.

"They're a handful," he said, looking over.

"*Jah*, but much better than they were. When I first came, they were totally out of control."

"Eb really has taken on his responsibilities. It's made a big difference."

"I can see that."

"So, it wasn't so bad today, was it? You seemed to have a lot to talk about with Hazel."

"She did most of the talking."

"Oh?"

"*Jah*, she said she really appreciated your allowing her to cry on your shoulder."

"She said that?"

"*Jah*. So, did she cry on your shoulder, Paul?"

He coughed and laughed awkwardly at the same time. "I don't remember that happening. She was upset one time about Jeremiah, but it didn't amount to much. You know how *maedel* can get."

"Paul, did you hold her in your arms? Tell me the truth."

"Now, why would you ask such a question?"

"Paul?"

He shuffled his feet and looked away. "Maybe for a second. Just in a friendly way."

"Paul? Is that the whole truth? You didn't go further, did you?"

"Further?"

"*Jah*, you know. Like a kiss?"

"Gee, it was a while ago…"

"Certainly, you'd remember if you kissed the girl!"

"I don't think that could have happened."

Martha leaped off the sofa and glared at him. "You did! You kissed her! You say you love me, but you end up kissing another girl! One you cared about once! She was way more than a friend back then, and maybe more now!"

"Now, Martha, you'll wake up the *kinner*. Settle down and we'll have a nice talk—"

"I don't think so! You can leave right now! I think you are having second thoughts! That's what I think!

And when I call and you don't answer, I think I know why now!"

"It was just one moment of weakness, Martha! Please listen. I know it was wrong. She came on me so strong—even letting her hair down, and—"

"Hair down? That tramp! How could you be attracted to such a brazen woman! Haven't you got any control?"

"I know. I know. It was a terrible mistake. I was just so lonely and she pushed it, Martha. I swear, the moment it happened, I hated myself for it. It will never happen again. I promise you."

"It's too late for promises, Paul. I'll never trust you again."

"Honey, please, don't talk like this. I love you. Only you! I want to marry you—now. Even if we have to live apart, at least we'd be man and wife."

"Oh, what a wonderful marriage that would be! Please go. I honestly don't know how I feel about you at this moment. All I know is, you've betrayed me, and for a hussy! She should leave the Amish. I have a good mind to go see your bishop and tell him what happened."

"Martha, calm down. You're making way too much out of this. It was wrong, we were both at fault, but we know it was a mistake."

"Oh, I think she doesn't see it as a mistake! She's using poor Jeremiah as a way to see you. Don't you have a brain? It's so obvious! She's going to break his heart, just as you're breaking mine! Maybe Daniel isn't so bad, after all."

"You can't mean that!"

"Oh no? You'd better leave now, Paul, before I really tell you what I feel!"

"Goodness sakes. There's more?" He rose from the sofa and went over to the peg for his hat. Before leaving, he turned back and looked into her eyes. "You're making a huge mistake, Martha. We have something very special together. For one stupid moment on my part, you're willing to throw it all away. Please pray about it and let yourself calm down. And please don't get ideas about Daniel. That would be foolish."

"Go. Just go." Her voice had softened somewhat, but the words tumbled out through trembling lips. As soon as she heard the door close, she burst into tears and sobbed uncontrollably. It was over. Her dream was destroyed. She had no intention of falling into a relationship with Daniel. In fact, she was done with men! Totally finished! She'd do missionary work in China or Africa. That was what she'd do!

The hours dragged Monday morning as Paul and Jeremiah worked side-by-side drawing up plans for their newest project. The man who was ordering the wall of shelving and cabinets was going to stop by on his way home from work to sign the papers and leave a deposit.

"You're awful quiet today, Paul. Everything okay?"

"Not really, but I can't talk about it right now."

"Martha?"

He nodded.

"She didn't seem like herself. Even Hazel mentioned that she was sharp with her. That's not like her."

"*Jah*, I'm sure Hazel's real concerned," he said sarcastically.

"What do you mean by that?"

"Sorry. Nothing, really. I'm just messed up right now.

I don't want to discuss it. So, you think we're charging enough for this? You know it's a huge wall."

"*Jah*, but I worked it out. You can check my figures."

"That's not necessary."

"Last night, I asked Hazel to marry me, Paul."

"Congratulations," he responded unenthusiastically.

"She didn't give me an answer yet."

"Too bad."

"What's going on? That's a weird thing to say."

"No, I mean it. It's too bad she can't make a decision. You're a great guy. She should be excited to have you care enough to marry her."

"Well, I told her I'd like an answer soon, so we can make plans for the fall. We've both been baptized, so that won't be a problem."

"Can we talk about something else?"

"Sure, buddy. In fact, we don't have to talk at all. I'm about ready for some more coffee. How about you?"

"No, not now. I'm going for a walk. Iron out some of my feelings." He put his tools down and walked past Ben, who was sawing shelves for another, smaller project. He was wearing ear protectors and wasn't able to hear what was being said. He merely nodded over as Paul left the building.

Paul walked quickly and then broke into a run. It felt good to concentrate on something besides Martha. He'd hurt her so badly without meaning to. His guilt had kept him awake most of the night. She'd left early the next day without leaving a message for him. Not that he expected anything. He feared he might never hear from her again.

What could he do to make up for such a terrible mistake? Hazel did it on purpose. The whole thing.

He should tell Jeremiah the truth about the girl before he actually married her. It would be difficult, but he couldn't let his friend be bamboozled by a woman like her. Jeremiah was too nice a guy.

Paul decided to pray about it first and ask God to help him use the right words. Then, after a few days, perhaps he'd try to write to Martha and convince her to forgive him. Hopefully, she wouldn't fall back on that Daniel guy. He was nothing but a phony. A wave of jealousy swarmed through his whole body. The thought of her marrying Daniel and bearing his children was almost more than he could stand. To think he'd compromised Martha and his future for a moment's pleasure. What a fool he'd been.

After running for over two miles, he turned back to the shop. There were two buggies parked in front. When he entered through the back door, he found Hazel sitting at their small kitchen table, a mug in one hand and a newspaper in the other. He could see Jeremiah in the showroom talking to a young couple. Ben was out collecting boards for a new project. He and Hazel were alone.

"Hi," she said, looking up.

"Hi."

"You're all sweaty."

"I know. I ran." Paul walked past her and picked up a clean rag and wiped off his forehead.

"Martha get home okay?"

"I wouldn't know."

Hazel's eyebrows rose. "Problems?"

"Perhaps, and maybe you know why." He turned towards her and stood several feet away as he glared over. "Could it have been something you told her, Hazel?

Maybe comments about a certain bench and using me for a crying board?"

"Now, Paul, I didn't say anything that wasn't the truth."

"Through your eyes. You know you just about seduced me that night. Shameful!"

She giggled. "Like you didn't enjoy it."

"I can't believe you get pleasure out of messing with people's lives. You know I'm going to tell Jeremiah what kind of person you've become."

Her laughter turned to anger. "You stay out of our lives, Paul. You wrecked mine once already, don't mess with Jeremiah and me."

"So, you did all this out of vengeance. What kind of Amish girl are you? You really don't belong in our community. Go with the English way of living. You'd fit right in with some of the young people I've met."

"You're wrong about me, Paul. I just go after what I want, and you've been the one I've wanted for as long as I can remember."

"It's over and has been for some time now."

"If you hadn't met Martha, we'd be married by now."

"I broke off with you even before I met her. I guess my spirit warned me even before I realized why I couldn't love you."

"Ridiculous! You did love me. Here comes Jeremiah. I warn you…"

"Leave him alone," he whispered hoarsely as Jeremiah came through the door, a big grin on his face.

"Hey, Paul, we just got another job! Things are really moving." Then he sat next to Hazel and reached for her hand. She looked over adoringly at him.

"You're such a fabulous salesman, Jeremiah. I'm soooo proud of you."

Paul nearly *kutzed*. The girl was incredible. There was no way he'd let her marry his best friend and ruin his life. Difficult as it would be, when they closed shop, he'd lay it all before him. To think, he'd even considered marrying the girl!

Oh, Martha, Martha, my dearest...

Chapter Twenty-One

Martha barely spoke to her driver. He rambled on about…heaven knows what. She found mild comfort in the resonance of his deep voice and nodded occasionally if he glanced over for a response, but her thoughts were centered on her life—her future. What lay ahead? Everything looked bleak.

Not only could she lose her mother, the woman who had raised her, loved her, comforted her through her childhood trials, but now she had no future hopes of a marriage with the man she had at one point cherished. How could she have been so wrong about someone? She truly believed they had something special. And now she found out he'd been unfaithful to her. How could she ever trust him again? And Hazel. Some friend she turned out to be.

Who could she trust? *Aenti* Liz? She was wrapped up with her own children and grandchildren. Yes, she loved her, but her aunt always saw things through the eyes of her sister. And her father, dear as he was, had enough on his mind with worrying about his wife…he sure didn't need to have his daughter to worry about as well.

There was Daniel, though she was never able to eliminate her feelings of distrust. She might never feel comfortable with him again. There was something about Daniel that gave her an uneasy feeling, as if he was not who he pretended to be.

Martha looked over at her driver, realizing he was asking her a question. "Sorry, what did you say?"

"I just remarked, we're nearly back to your home already."

"Oh, you're right. I hadn't noticed."

"So, when are you and Paul going to announce your wedding?"

"I don't know," she said, not wishing to talk about Paul, or anyone else. The tears were too close. She needed to be alone to think, and certainly discussing Paul with her driver was not a good option.

He went back to telling her about his trip to Canada and she went back to her own thoughts. Finally, he pulled into her drive and she got out and paid him. "Just let me know when you need me again, and I'll try to work it out so you get more time. I had my plans all set up to help my buddy with his new house construction this afternoon. His windows were being delivered this morning."

"It's okay. I was ready to come home anyway," she said as he reached into the trunk for her overnight bag. After he took off, she went into the house. It was quiet. She wondered if her parents were even home, though she'd noticed their covered buggy was back in the barn area. She noted the open buggy was gone.

As she began to unpack, she heard her mother call

out from her bedroom. Martha opened the door to her mother's room and found the shades drawn and her mother in bed.

"I just got home, *Mamm*. Are you feeling sickly?"

"*Jah*. I'm afraid it's been a rough couple of days without you. I'm so glad you're home. Come sit beside me."

Martha obeyed her, though her heart was so broken, it was difficult to feel any emotion, even toward this woman who meant so much to her.

"How did it go with your visit?" she asked Martha.

"Okay. The children are getting big."

"I bet the twins are adorable."

"*Jah*, they are."

"And Paul? How's he doing?"

"Fine."

"You sound sad, Martha. Are you okay?"

"Not really, *Mamm*, but I don't want to talk about it right now."

"Maybe it would help."

"*Nee*. Can I get you anything?"

"I'm okay. Your father went to get me some more medicine for the nausea. He should be home soon. Lizzy brings food over."

"Have you been in bed the whole time I was gone?"

"Pretty much. I feel real weak, but at least I don't go back for a while for more chemo. I get a little break."

"I'm glad."

"I think I'll sleep now, knowing you're home safe."

"You shouldn't worry about me, *Mamm*. I'm all grown up now."

"I'll always worry about my little *maed*, even when you're an old lady of forty," she said with a weak smile.

Martha leaned over and kissed her cheek. Then she

left the room and went to her own room, collapsed on her bed and allowed the tears to flow. Her world was crashing all about her. At that moment, she thought of the woman who had given birth to her. How traumatic her life had been. A young Amish woman, carried away by her emotions with a man from another country—half a world away. What horrible guilt she must have felt to have succumbed to her feelings. And then to discover she was carrying his child. She must have been devastated. Would he have married her, if he'd known she was pregnant? Would he have returned from Italy once he found out? The young girl had so little choice in the whole matter. Her father wouldn't allow her to raise the child herself. It must have torn her apart to go through nine months and the birth, and then have to give her child to another. Had she loved her baby?

Martha ceased crying and pictured the moment when her mother had handed her over to Sarah. It tore at her as she revisited that devastating moment through the eyes of her birth mother. And now after all those years, Rose Esh had found a way to contact her. She'd suffered all those years, wondering about her daughter, and now all she wanted was to meet her. To be reassured she'd done the right thing.

Martha climbed off her bed and opened the drawer where she'd hidden the information about her mother's whereabouts. She would write back and perhaps they could meet briefly. She had written that she was free to travel. If she was serious about returning to Lancaster in order to see her, this would be the opening.

After rereading the short letter, Martha took a pad of paper from the table beside her bed and began a letter in response. With all the pain she was enduring, perhaps this would be a light in her future.

It was quitting time. Paul and Jeremiah had already told Ben to take off for the rest of the day. They felt they'd caught up enough with their orders to close up around five for a change. After cleaning the tools they'd used and setting them in their proper places, Jeremiah headed for the door.

"Wait, Jeremiah. I need to talk to you," Paul blurted out.

Jeremiah turned, questioning with his eyes. "We ain't talked enough for one day?" he asked with a faint smile.

"I really have to talk to you about something personal. It's serious, I'm afraid."

Jeremiah's smile dissolved and he came back into the work area. "Should I be sitting?"

Paul nodded and they sat at the small table where they often had coffee. Paul cleared his throat. "It's about Hazel."

"What about her?"

"I don't know where to begin."

Jeremiah shrugged. "At the beginning."

"I guess I don't have to go back that far. You know we were going together a while back."

"And you broke it off, because of Martha."

"Not quite true. I had broken off before I even met Martha, because I realized I didn't really love Hazel. Not enough to marry her, anyway."

"And she never really got over you. Is that what you want to tell me? Because I already know that and we've talked about it."

"She's still trying to get me, Jeremiah."

"Oh, come on, Paul."

"I'm serious. When I was having problems with Martha and we didn't see each other much, Hazel took full advantage of it. She did everything she could to get me back."

"Like what?"

"Like coming on to me. Strong. She even put her hair down and made me kiss her."

"Made you? She forced you? Really?" His eyes burned as he stared at his friend.

"Okay, I was weak. I have to admit, she's a real attractive *maed* and I was lonely—so much so that I forgot myself and we kissed."

Jeremiah slammed his fist on the table and his jaw was rigid. "You've both betrayed me! How could you? Look at us—we're partners! I thought we were best of friends! And Hazel—she's a tramp!" He rose from the table and stomped out of the building. Paul remained in his seat, immobile. The door to the house Jeremiah was living in slammed shut so hard, it reverberated in the quiet of the evening. Had he made a mistake in telling Jeremiah everything? He wondered now if it had been for his friend's sake, or his own, to expose the woman Hazel had become. How many lives were wrecked at this point? Perhaps his own pain in losing Martha had blinded him to how his confession would affect others. Too late. It was out there—for good or otherwise. Where would it all end?

Chapter Twenty-Two

So far, today had proven to be an unproductive day for Rose Esh. It started out with a leak discovered under the kitchen sink, which resulted, not only in an unexpected plumbing bill, but a nasty mess of wet boxes of detergents and cleaning supplies. A writing deadline hung over her head, and the three hours she'd spent writing the day before turned out to have been in vain. After cleaning the mess from the leak, she eliminated the last six pages of her manuscript and began again.

Around noon, she decided to take a break and enjoy the beautiful June day. The sky was nearly cloudless, the deepest blue she'd seen since the previous summer, and flowers were bursting in everyone's well-tended yard as she walked through the pleasant neighborhood. One neighbor waved to her as she planted annuals in her small garden to the side of her brick ranch home. In spite of all the beauty in her world, Rose was preoccupied with her personal problems. She had accepted the fact that she wouldn't hear from her daughter. Too much time had passed.

Her only hope was that Martha had not yet returned

to the ice cream parlor where her letter lay in wait. She fully trusted the young clerk to present it to her when, and if, the occasion arose. The worst scenario, which creeped into her consciousness too frequently, would be that the note was in her daughter's hands and either put aside indefinitely or destroyed. Who could blame her? All these years had passed without a word. How many times she'd wanted to check on her daughter's welfare, but she had to live up to her promise. And that she had done.

When she got back home, she opened her mailbox to collect her bills and advertisements. There were several pieces of mail in her stack and she waited until she got in the house before checking through them. As she sat at the kitchen table, she ripped up the annoying ads and put aside her electric bill. Then she discovered a handwritten letter. Her heart began to pound as she checked the return address carefully printed in the left upper hand corner. Could it be? *Paradise, Pennsylvania.*

She ripped it open quickly and removed the two pages and unfolded them. The printing was neatly done with a black pen. It was difficult at first to read the words since her eyes had filled with unshed tears. She wiped them with a paper napkin and began to read aloud—almost afraid of what might be shared on these stark white sheets of paper.

> *"Hi. This is from Martha Troyer. I understand that I was adopted twenty years ago when I was a little baby. I also heard that you were the person who gave birth to me. I learned about it not long ago and then I got your letter, so I know it is true. I was not told about the adoption until re-*

cently. It was a bit of a shock, I can tell you. But I am used to the idea now.

"*I think it is nice that you write books about Amish people and it wonders me if you might be sorry you aren't Amish anymore. I would like to meet you sometime if you come back to Pennsylvania, but I would not expect you to pay all that money to come out just for that.*

"*I can't send you a picture of how I look all grown up, because I don't have any pictures. But I can tell you that I do not look Amish. I have very dark hair and eyes and I saw a picture of my father and I think I look Italian like him. I also like pizza and even spaghetti. Of course, I like chicken and dumplings, too, so I guess I'm a mix.*

"*Thank you for thinking of me and writing to me. It means a lot to me. Especially right now, because the young Amishman that I was hoping to marry betrayed me and I can no longer marry him. Even if he wants that. I don't know if he does anymore. It hurts my heart pretty bad so if you like to pray, you can ask God to help me with my pain.*

"*I hope you are happy and healthy and continue to write good books. I want to go to the library when I have a chance and borrow one of your books.*

"*Sincerely,*
"*Martha Troyer*"

Rose held the letter against her breast and then, with shaking hands, reread it. She tried to picture her daughter as she wrote the letter. It revealed so much. She sounded as if she'd forgiven her. That was clearly what meant the most to Rose. Someday she hoped to hear the words spoken. Martha had also exposed some of her inner thoughts and even asked for prayer. That showed trust, something she hadn't yet earned. Was there an unseen connection between a mother and her child, even when distance and circumstances divided them? It saddened her to know Martha was suffering from a broken heart. What kind of man would betray a sweet innocent woman, whom he planned to wed? It angered her to know the pain he caused her dear daughter.

Rose removed her calendar from the wall and checked her obligations for the next several weeks. If only she didn't have the manuscript to complete. She was only halfway through, and not happy with it at that. Her editor was strict with the timing and since she was under contract, she could not postpone her submission. But that project should be completed by the end of June. Halfway through July, she had a two-week segment marked off. Every year at that time, she vacationed at the Jersey shore with two of her single friends, whom she had met in college. One gal had never married, but the other was recently divorced. They'd be disappointed if Rose didn't show up, but if she explained she was going to meet her daughter, whom they didn't even know existed, surely, they'd understand. Yes, that would be the time. Just to be sure, she wondered if she should write back to Martha first. But what fun to surprise her! The chances of the young woman being anywhere but at home were slim.

She looked at the return address again. Now she had an address. She traced it with her forefinger. Alas, it was a rural number not a street address, so that ruled out a surprise visit. She'd organize her plans and write back once things were firmed up on her end, to make sure it was amenable to Martha. It would be quicker to fly, but then she'd have to rent a car. No, she'd drive out when the time came. What had started out as a dismal day was now one of the happiest of her entire life! What a difference a letter can make.

Melvin held his wife in his arms and kissed the side of her head. "You asleep yet?"

"If I had been, I sure ain't now," Sarah said with a soft chuckle.

"I've been so busy lately, I haven't spent much time with you, is all."

"I know, honey. I understand. I've been married to you long enough to know how hard it is in the spring getting everything done."

"I feel like I'm finally caught up. If you're feeling *gut* enough, maybe we can spend the day at a zoo or something tomorrow. Would you like that?"

"It's sweet of you to think of it, but I'm really too wore out to spend all that time on my feet. Maybe we could just go out for lunch."

"Whatever you'd like, dear. At least you're not *kutzing* now."

"*Nee*, I get a break for another week. Then it starts all over."

"You're very brave, you know."

"What choice do I have? I want to get all better. I sure don't want some other woman coming in here and telling you what to do."

"I'll never marry again, Sarah. *Gott* forbid I'm alone someday, I'll always have Martha."

"She sure don't talk about marriage now. Poor thing. She looks so sad most of the time."

"Whatever happened with her and Paul?"

"I don't know. She won't talk about it."

"I hope she didn't break up because of us wanting her to stay home."

"I don't think so. Lizzy tried to get her to talk, but she clams right up. Every day I see her watch for the mail, but I guess he hasn't written because she comes in with that sad face of hers. Breaks my heart."

"Maybe Daniel will get her to smile again."

"He hasn't been here in quite a while."

"Guess he has a lot of work to do."

"Or a new girl."

"I doubt that. He's been pretty smitten with our *dochder* for some time now."

"It would be nice if they got together, except I have a hard time liking his family. They're so stiff and mean looking."

He smiled in the dark. "Maybe I'll try to talk to Martha tomorrow."

"She's pretty closemouthed about everything right now, Melvin. You may just want to save your breath."

"*Jah*, she's never been one to open up much to me. I know she loves me, but it's you she can talk to, I guess."

"Well, women talk, you know. I was the same with my *mudder*. My *daed* scared me a wee bit, though he was kind to me."

"I bet Lizzy was the one to get into trouble."

"Oh, *jah*, for sure. She had a mouth on her."

"Still does, if you ask me."

"You just don't understand her. She's got a big heart."

"Just hides it," he said. "Now, I should let you get some sleep. If you're up to it, I'll take you to that fancy buffet tomorrow for lunch."

"That's pretty pricey," she said.

"Don't you worry about it. We have the money. Sometimes, you have to splurge a little. You're worth every penny, Sarah. You're the best."

She snuggled against her strong husband. He was a rock. First was God, second was her Melvin, and third was her Martha. There were too many times when she got the order mixed up and put Martha on top. That had to end. The girl was a woman now and she knew she had to loosen the apron strings and let Martha be the woman God intended her to be.

Chapter Twenty-Three

Paul paced back and forth across the showroom. It had been more than a week since Martha had left him. Now he not only had the pain of her leaving, but Jeremiah hadn't shown up for work since the day he talked to him about Hazel.

Paul had stopped at his family's farm and they had no idea he was even missing, presuming he was at his new home. Finally, he'd even made his way to Eb and Deborah's to see if Deb could ask Hazel about Jeremiah. They knew nothing either, and told him they hadn't even seen Hazel during that period of time.

Certainly, they hadn't taken off somewhere together! But where were they? Ben seemed upset at his boss's absence as well, but Paul had nothing to say to alleviate his concerns. They kept the place together as well as they could, but they were beginning to get backed up. It was difficult to concentrate. He hadn't even written to Martha, since he got home so late each night, it was all he could do to get his teeth brushed and clean up from work.

Ben came into the showroom and showed him the

color of stain he'd put on a sample piece of wood in preparation for staining a rocker. "What do you think? Too dark?"

"It's okay," Paul said, barely glancing at the wood. "Look, I need to run an errand. Can you handle everything yourself for a while?"

"I'll try. I've never worked with customers, though."

"Then I'll close the showroom. No one's been in today, anyway. I think it's too hot for people to be out shopping. Why don't you take the rest of the day off?"

"We have too much to do, Paul. I wouldn't feel right."

Paul sighed. "You're probably right. Okay, forget I said that. I'll probably be back within the hour."

He started out in his buggy, slowly at first. The last thing he wanted was to see Hazel again, but he hadn't gone to her home yet to ask about Jeremiah. He'd keep his distance, for sure. He wasn't about to complicate his life any more than it was, and he had absolutely no interest in pursuing any kind of relationship with that girl. He was shocked when he thought about how she'd turned into such a disgraceful Amish woman. He'd never met anyone like her. He tried to downplay his part in the scandalous event.

As he pulled up the drive, his eye went to a thin, tall man, pushing a wheelbarrow filled with mulch towards a garden patch. It was Jeremiah! Paul was filled with relief, followed by curiosity. What on earth was he doing at Hazel's home?

Jeremiah stopped walking and set the handles down. He placed his hands on his hips and watched as Paul secured the reins on a post and jumped down. When he got close, Paul shook his head. "You sure had me worried. What on earth are you doing here?"

"I'm staying with my fiancé till I figure out what I'm going to do with the business."

"Fiancé? Are you serious? After all I told you?"

"Look, Paul, I know you believe anything Martha tells you, but the girl is lying. Hazel loves me and we're going to get married in October. It's all arranged."

"And you think I lied to you, too? About her coming on to me?"

"Maybe you just read her wrong. She's not that kind of girl. She's a sweet innocent *maed* and I love her and she loves me. Only me."

Paul shook his head. "I can't believe this. And what do you mean about the business? We work well together, don't we?"

"I'm fed up with everyone and everything. I like farming. Her *daed*'s been wonderful to me. He wants me to stay here after we're married and help out. We can sell the business, or you can buy it out from me."

"Good grief! You've been hypnotized! Do you know what you're saying?"

"Sure do."

Paul heard the screen door squeak as it opened and he could see Hazel out of the corner of his eye heading straight for them. When she reached Jeremiah's side, she put her hand around his waist. "*Hallo*, Paul."

He nodded, frowning at the same time.

"Did Jeremiah tell you the *gut* news?"

"*Jah.*"

"I hope you can be happy for us. *Gott* has brought us together and we couldn't be happier." She smiled up at Jeremiah, who leaned over and kissed the tip of her nose.

"Oh, naughty. Not in front of people. You know how embarrassed I get."

Paul had had enough. He shook his head and turned towards the buggy. "Come to the shop tomorrow, Jeremiah. We have a lot to discuss."

"I'll try to get over."

Paul looked back and glared at him. "There's more at stake here than your marriage. We have a contract."

"I guess I can make it. Sometime in the afternoon, though. I have cows to milk and chickens to feed."

"I'm sure you do." Paul climbed in and without another word, headed for the street.

No one can say Paul didn't warn him. The guy seemed to have flipped mentally. Hazel had a way about her and men could be fooled by a pretty face. Heaven knows, he almost made a huge mistake. As it was, his relationship with Martha was tenuous, at best. He refused to give up. They had too much going for them, for a foolish mistake to ruin something that special? Well, he couldn't stand by and do nothing. Letters she could destroy even without reading them. A phone call, even if he was able to make one—she could end by hanging up. He'd just go and pay her a visit. He'd stay out in the barn if she wouldn't let him in the house. Yup, he'd park himself down and wait until she softened and would listen to him. If it took three days or three months, he was not about to give up on the woman he so dearly loved.

When could he leave though? Business had piled up, especially since Jeremiah decided to take a vacation. Though he was relieved that nothing terrible had happened, he couldn't help but feel upset with the guy. As he pulled into the business lot, he saw Ben unloading wood into the storeroom. There was a good worker. He never stopped. There weren't many men like him anymore. You'd think he was Amish, Paul thought to himself as he headed over to give him a hand.

When Ben asked about Jeremiah, Paul tried to answer as truthfully as he could without divulging the argument that caused him to leave in the first place. He mentioned Jeremiah's engagement.

"Huh, I don't know if I'd trust that woman," Ben said, scowling.

"Why do you say that?"

"I hate to mention it and I won't tell Jeremiah, but I think she was trying to get me interested in her. She's a huge flirt when we've found ourselves alone."

"I know that about her and I tried to warn Jeremiah, but he won't listen. You'd be wasting your breath."

"Well, it's none of my business, I just hate to see the guy get hurt. He's a good person."

"I agree a hundred per cent. Though maybe once she marries, she'll settle down and be a *gut* housewife."

"I sure hope so." After a few moments of silence, Ben held up an eight-foot board. "This looks like quality wood, doesn't it? I think we should stick with this supplier. By the way, when do you expect Jeremiah to come back to work? I'm feeling the pressure."

"Hopefully, tomorrow. He's coming by to talk anyway. We'll need to talk privately, Ben. No offense."

"None taken. I can work outside if he shows up or try handling the showroom. I guess I should learn how to do that as well."

"True, and we'd be nearby if you needed us. Thanks for all you do, Ben. We really appreciate it."

"Hey, you pay me. I just try to give you a good day's work for a good day's pay."

Martha checked the sheets on the line. They were already dry, and they'd only been out a couple of hours. Between the light breeze and the hot June sun, she was able to hang several loads out in one day. The winter quilts should have been laundered already, but too much was going on in her life and their laundering had been postponed till now.

Since her washing machine was the old wringer type, she hand washed the quilts to protect them from damage. Once they were rinsed sufficiently, she twisted and wrung the quilts out with her mother's aid until they had lost the bulk of the water. After removing the dry sheets, they hung the heavy quilts up together, placing multiple clothes pins to hold them in place.

As they worked, they heard a buggy coming down the gravel path towards the back yard.

"That may be Lizzy," Sarah said. "She wanted to come by and see your *dawdi* and *mammi*."

"I'll make some lemonade and maybe we can get everyone under the oak tree where it's shaded and take a break together."

"*Gut* idea," Sarah said. "I'm plum wore out from squeezing these things. Goodness, it's a lot of work."

"Go sit then, *Mamm*."

When the buggy appeared by the side of the building, it wasn't Lizzy. It was Daniel. It had been nearly a month since he'd made his last appearance, and Martha wasn't thrilled to see him. If he was a male, he was on her bad side, these days.

"Hey, Martha, where are you going?" he called after her as she continued to head for the back door.

"I'm getting lemonade. *Mamm*'s there. Go talk to her."

"Okay. Sure, I'll have some lemonade."

"Oh, did I ask you? I didn't hear myself, I guess," she said sarcastically. She'd take an extra few minutes to squeeze a couple lemons. Maybe he'd tire of her mother's conversation and leave. She had zero patience with him or anyone else of his gender. Well, her grandfather and father were still okay in her book, but that was it. Oh, and maybe the bishop.

Lizzy showed up several minutes later. She came in to help after saying hello to her sister and their guest.

"I'm fine, *Aenti*, why don't you go get your parents. It's too nice to be inside all day. *Dawdi* complains all winter about being stuck inside and then all summer, he fusses about the heat."

Lizzy laughed. "*Jah*, that's him all right. Okay, I'll go work on them and see you outside. Your *daed* is getting folding chairs from the barn with Daniel. I thought that boy would be around soon. Your *mudder* said he's been scarce lately. I'm sure if he knew you were a free woman now, he would have been around sooner."

"Don't tell him, please. I don't need him sugar talking me to death."

"Hmm. You sound like you've given up on all men. You used to like it when Paul talked sweet."

"We're done. Finished! I hope I never see him again."

"Someday, you're going to have to break down and tell your old *aenti* what happened. I'm a *gut* listener."

"I know. I'm sorry, but I don't even like to think about what happened. I'm still hurting pretty bad over it. Maybe someday. By the way, don't tell *Mamm*, but I wrote to my birth *mudder*."

"Well, I'll be. How about that?"

"I told her I'd like to meet her, too, but I don't want *Mamm* to know anything about it. I'm afraid she'd be upset and I don't want to hurt her. I just think I'm ready to see the woman. I do have some questions."

"I'm sure. I understand, honey. And no, I won't say a word to anyone. Not even your *onkel*, but I'll want to hear all about it."

"You don't think it's wrong for me to get in touch with her then?"

"Of course not. It's normal for you to be curious. It won't change anything about your feelings for my *schwester*, I know."

"*Nee*. It couldn't."

"Did your *mudder* tell you she wants to let you use a cell phone now so you can talk to Paul as often as you want? She plans to mention it to your *daed*."

"It's a little late for that. We aren't speaking to each other, at all."

"Oh, Martha, why not? What on earth happened?"

"I guess I may as well tell you. I found out he was cheating on me."

"No! I can't believe it!"

"He admitted it."

"Was it a serious thing?"

"To me it was very serious. We had an understanding. We were to marry." Martha's voice started to crack as she broke down for the first time to tell anyone the story. "He said he loved me and then I found out he went back to the other girl he used to date—Hazel—and she let her hair down and they kissed! Can you believe it?"

"Wait, isn't Hazel the sister of Deborah? The girl you went to help?"

"That's her. They had dated before I met him, but it was supposed to be over. Oh, *Aenti* Liz, my heart is broken." She wept as her aunt took her in her arms.

"Hush, dear, it ain't the end of the world. He's only one man."

"But he's the man I love—loved. How could he do that?"

"Did you ask him?"

"Oh *jah*, and he admitted it happened. He said it was a mistake."

"*Jah*, I'd have to agree with him on that."

"And that it would never happen again. He said he still loves me, but how can I ever trust him now?"

"Maybe that girl was mainly at fault. Some women are really bad. They are like tramps. She may have pushed him when he was weak."

"Of course, that's his excuse. How weak can you be?"

"Mmm. Pretty weak sometimes. Listen to me. Once after I was married about two years, your *onkel* took a friend of mine to an auction and afterwards she invited him back to her house for a cup of coffee. He said he didn't think it would be wrong, so he went. Once he was there, she told him she was in love with him and wanted him to be her boyfriend. Can you imagine? He was married—to me. See, there are some bad people out there. It took me a while to believe nothing happened, but then I figured it could happen to any man and I'd have to accept what he said. The day it happened, he said nothing went on, and he left right away."

"But he left! Paul stayed—long enough to kiss her! That's horrible!"

"*Jah*, I agree, but maybe in time he can prove he still loves you."

"He hasn't written to me."

"Mmm. Not *gut*. And no calls?"

"I'd have to call him, and I'm not about to do that."

"Maybe he'll show up some day."

"I hope not. I don't want to ever see him again."

"I think you still care."

A new flood of tears. "*Jah*, I'll always love him, but I don't want to see him."

"Honey, in time you'll get over this. You pray about it."

"I do. Every night."

"And doesn't that help?"

"It helps, but my heart is still in pieces. I don't think it will ever be better again."

"Now, maybe you need to be nicer to Daniel. He's not that bad, and I'm sure he still cares about you."

"That's not going to happen. I just can't make myself love the man. He's attractive and he treats me *gut* now, though I don't know how long that would last, but I just can't get over my feelings for Paul, even though I'm mad at him."

"Time. Everything takes time. Now go wash your face. I'll take out the pitcher of lemonade and you can bring some glasses when you come out. Be nice to Daniel, anyway. He's a guest in your home and you're a proper young Amish woman who respects her company, even when you don't like them real well." She winked as Martha wiped her eyes on her apron and headed for the bathroom.

"*Danki*, *Aenti* Liz. I don't know what I'd do without you."

"Me neither," she said, smiling gently at her niece.

Chapter Twenty-Four

It was two in the afternoon before Jeremiah sauntered into the showroom and made his way back to the workshop where Ben and Paul were adjusting the framework for a large cherry bookcase. He stood watching for several minutes while they struggled with the sheer weight of the piece as they shimmied the case against a wall to await cabinet doors and shelving.

When it was securely in place, Ben mentioned he was ready for a late lunch break, and headed outside to their picnic table, which they used in good weather.

Jeremiah nodded towards the bookcase. "You're doing a nice job. Couldn't do better myself."

"We could use your help, you know. It would be nice if you could separate your personal life from your business life. You can't stay away forever."

Jeremiah sat down on one of the side chairs and motioned for Paul to join him. "Now I know you think I'm crazy to be marrying Hazel—"

"It's none of my business, Jeremiah. I told you what I thought you needed to know, and you've disregarded it, so all I can do is hope things work out for you. I'm real sincere in wanting the best for you—and Hazel. I'm sorry I got involved with her again, even though it was brief and just a moment of bad thinking on my part."

"And hers. She explained that she was pretty shaken up after you grabbed her, but she forgave you right away. She knows you were lonely and just not yourself."

"She said I grabbed *her*?"

"I know you'll argue about the details, but I don't want to hear them. Hazel and I don't discuss it anymore. We're real happy and excited for the wedding to take place, and I hope you and Martha will come to wish us well."

"Sure, we would be happy to, if we're together by then."

"So, you think we can put all this stuff behind us and work together again?"

"I know I can. I'd hope you could as well. When you disappeared, I was pretty worried about you, you know."

"I guess I should have let people know where I was. I just needed to get over my anger first. I know it's time to get back to business, though. I'll come in tomorrow and get started again. Tell me how far you guys have gotten with our projects."

After discussing business for about an hour, Jeremiah picked up his straw hat and headed for the door. Before he pushed it open, he turned with a glint in his eyes. "I don't really like farming, you know. If I'd had to muck one more stall, I think I would have thrown a rope over a tree and made myself a noose."

Paul laughed. He nodded. "I know the feeling."

Paul decided to wait a couple of days before taking off for Paradise. It was important to get caught up with their jobs, and it would give Martha a little more time to cool off. He could foresee one other potential problem. Jeremiah and Hazel would be their closest neighbors. Good thing they were all Amish. They *had* to live in harmony. No other option left.

Rose read over the letter she had written for Martha. It was her third attempt, and though she wasn't totally satisfied with some of the wording, she decided it was good enough to send. She mentioned the two weeks in July as being the best time for her to travel and asked if that would be convenient for Martha. Not wanting to sound as if she planned to monopolize Martha's time, she asked what day might be the most advantageous for their meeting and then suggested having lunch out at a quiet restaurant of Martha's choosing.

Hopefully, she'd hear back quickly so she could make her plans. It was already mid-June.

After sealing the envelope, she placed it in her mailbox and lifted the flag. She had already spoken on the phone with her friends whom she vacationed with each year. This time, she opened up to her closest friend, Doris, who was overwhelmed by the news. She wasn't the least judgmental, leaving Rose wondering why she had kept her child a secret all these years.

Doris made her promise to take pictures, though Rose explained how the Amish usually avoided having their pictures taken.

"Sneak it, then," Doris said. "I have to see if she looks like you."

"She took after her father. I could tell when she was born with her flock of nearly black hair. She was a beautiful baby, Doris. I'll never forget her dear little rosebud lips. You can't imagine how difficult it was to give her to someone else to raise. My penance, I guess."

"Maybe now you can make up for some of those lost years."

"I'm not counting on anything. I just need to know she's happy, and that she's forgiven me."

"She wouldn't be a woman of good character to be angry after all these years."

"Her letter sounded like she's accepted the whole situation."

"Will you see the people who adopted her while you're there?"

"I don't know. I haven't gotten that far to ask. I'll play it by ear. I would like to see them, if just to thank them for raising Martha."

"I hope they treated her right."

"I'm sure they did. Martha bonded to the woman immediately. It was amazing. You can tell Peg my story. I'd call her, too, but I don't know how she'd respond, and I don't want anything said which might make me any more nervous than I already am."

"I know what you're saying. Well, we'll miss you, but this is far more important than lying on a beach all day dredging yourself in sunscreen."

"I'm glad you understand."

"Absolutely! Have a wonderful time and be sure to call me when you get back."

After she hung up, Rose sat back on the sofa and tried to picture what their first meeting would be like. It could go in any direction, but her fervent prayer was that they would have some kind of bonding and that they'd find something in common to talk about.

It was foolish to try to predict the future. Rose finished her cup of coffee and returned to her computer to delve into her latest manuscript. Writing was not only a means of making a living, but her escape from reality as well.

Sarah felt stronger with each passing day, though she knew it was short-lived with the prospects of another bout of chemo lurking only a week away. The new medication had been more effective with her nausea and vomiting, controlling it significantly. A big improvement over years before when she'd conquered her other cancer.

She felt more optimistic about the outcome as time went on. She took time to enjoy her life and the glorious summer days and spent a few hours outside the days it was cool enough. It was her favorite time of year. She and Martha worked in the vegetable garden early in the mornings before the sun became too strong. They often sang hymns together as they worked. Martha seemed more like herself as time went on, though after she collected the mail each day, there was a period where she would go off by herself for an hour or longer, and there were other times when Sarah noticed her daughter's eyes were red and her lids were swollen. It pained her to see her daughter suffering, but she had not shared her break-up with Sarah as of yet. So, she no longer asked. When it was time, Martha would confide in her, as she always had in the past. They were close friends as well as mother and daughter.

Daniel had stopped by for a few minutes the day before, but only to leave off a batch of macaroons his sister had made for Sarah. He barely talked to Martha, who tried to avoid him altogether. Sarah no longer held out hopes of them marrying, and feared her daughter had been so disillusioned by the young men in her life, that she'd remain single. At one time, that might have pleased Sarah, but no longer. After much prayer and thought, she realized she had been too possessive of Martha and she was now prepared to rejoice with Martha if she and Paul reunited and decided to marry—even if it meant moving. After all, it wasn't that far away.

A friend of hers just told her that her only son had recently left the Amish and was going out to Michigan to live with a young woman he'd met at the grocery store! Mercy! What gets into these young people? Her friend was heartbroken. It made Sarah realize she should be thankful her daughter was going to remain Amish and still live in the same state.

"I need a break, *Mamm*," Martha said, wiping her brow. She gathered a few of their tools and set them under a shed roof. "Let's go see *Mammi* and *Dawdi*. I bet she has fresh iced tea made."

"*Jah*, she always does. Sure, I'm sick of pulling weeds anyway. They'll just pop up new tomorrow."

They walked over and knocked on the door and then let themselves in. *Dawdi* was working on a jigsaw puzzle on their card table next to a window in the sitting room while his wife was stirring pancake batter.

Martha and Sarah shared the sink to wash their hands.

"Just in time for some pancakes," *Mammi* said to her daughter.

"Not for us though, *Mamm*," Sarah said. "We had a large breakfast."

"I'm so happy to see you feeling so *gut*, Sarah,"

Mammi said. "I wish you were done with all that chemo."

"Me, too, but at least I get a few weeks between. This may be my last batch coming up. The doctor wants to run some tests in about a month."

"Ah. We'll pray for it to be done with then. You look *gut*, that's for sure. Don't she, Martha?"

"*Jah. Mamm*'s always beautiful to me." She put her arm around her mother and kissed the side of her head.

"Look, you're getting taller, Martha. You have to lean over more to reach my cheek," Sarah said, grinning.

"*Ach*. You're getting shorter, Sarah," *Mammi* said. "Soon you'll be my size. We can wear the same *fracks*."

The women laughed as *Dawdi* left the card table to join them in the kitchen. They sat and talked awhile about the weather and the growth of the crops. Then *Mammi* turned to Martha and asked about Paul. "Is he coming to see you soon?"

"I don't expect that will happen. I haven't been able to talk about it—I've been too upset, but I don't think I'll ever see him again."

"Oh, my goodness. You two seemed so smitten with each other. Whatever happened?"

Martha let out an exaggerated sigh. "I guess I may as well tell you all."

"Now if this is girl-talk, I'll go back to my puzzle," her grandfather informed them.

"*Jah*, go. Go," her *mammi* said, flitting her hand as if chasing a fly. "Men shouldn't listen to us when we talk about personal things."

"Humph." He made a quick exit and her grandmother

set a large pitcher of fresh sweet tea on the table and added three large plastic glasses.

Martha proceeded to tell them about Paul's episode of unfaithfulness. The women were shocked into silence. Finally, her grandmother clucked her tongue. "I guess he's begged to be forgiven."

"But how can I forgive him? We were planning to marry! He claimed he loved me." Martha was able to keep her tears at bay so far, but she felt all the heartbreak over again as she relayed his terrible transgression.

"That *maed* sounds like a hussy to me," Sarah said. "Imagine taking her hair down in front of someone she's not even married to. Shame on her."

"*Jah*, and kissing!" *Mammi* added. "Who ever heard of a man and woman kissing before their vows are said?"

Sarah looked over at her daughter, who was turning scarlet. If all was confessed, Sarah would have to admit she and Melvin had been slightly premature with their smooching as well—but it was history her family did not have to know about, for sure.

Mammi reached across the table and touched Martha's hand. "As an Amish woman, you need to forgive him, Martha."

"I can forgive, maybe, but I can't forget, and I can't marry a man I don't trust."

Sarah lowered her voice and the others leaned in to hear her words of wisdom. "Melvin had kissed another woman once before we got engaged. I learned about it from the woman herself. That Hazel sounds a lot like her. When I brought it up to Melvin, he confessed, but he swore it would never happen again, if we were married."

"And you believed him, obviously," Martha whispered.

"*Jah*, because I loved him enough to take my chances that he was telling the truth."

"I'm sure he's been faithful, *Mamm*," Martha said, nodding her head.

"I'm sure, too. We've had our moments, but I've never worried about it again. You can do the same Martha, if he makes that promise to you."

"Well, he hasn't even written to me, so I guess he really doesn't care that much. That's another reason I'm hurting so bad. At this point, he'd have to do a whole lot of sweet-talking to get me to even listen."

"And you're not interested in that Daniel, boy, at all?" *Mammi* asked.

"*Nee*. I'd rather be single for the rest of my life. In fact, I'm totally fed up with all guys."

"Poor dear," Sarah said, wiping her eyes. "I had no idea you were hurtin' so bad."

"I didn't want to trouble you, *Mamm*. You have enough going on right now."

"It might have helped to talk about it."

"I probably should have, but it's taken me this long to be able to talk about it without blubbering."

"*Jah*, we understand," *Mammi* said, stroking her hand. "You may not believe this now, but someday it will just seem like a bad dream, and I bet you will end up finding a real nice Amishman, who will treat you just right."

"I don't even care."

"No, but someday you will. Though look at old Mazie

Bender. She does just fine being single. Even though she's in her eighties now, she still quilts wonderful-*gut*. Don't even need thick glasses."

"*Jah, Mamm*," Sarah said, "she's an amazing woman and always full of smiles and happy thoughts. We should get by to see her, once I'm strong again."

"*Jah*, the three of us should go. Maybe four. I'll ask Lizzy to come along. Does Lizzy know about you and Paul?" *Mammi* asked.

Martha knew her mother wouldn't be pleased to know she'd talked about it with her aunt and not her, so she worded her answer very carefully.

"A little, only because she found me crying one day and got it out of me."

"Oh *jah*. That's my *schwester*," Sarah said. "She has to know everything that's going on."

"Now, Sarah, I'm sure she just wanted to help," her mother reminded her.

Martha nodded in agreement. "But you two are far better at helping me through this. *Danki* for listening."

"And did it make sense to you, Martha?" her grand-mother asked. "Are you going to listen to Paul if he calls?"

"I guess so, though he can't call me. I don't have a phone, remember?"

"I told you, I kept the phone we took away, Mar-tha," her mother reminded her. "I'll give it back to you if your *daed* agrees, and then maybe *you* can make the first call."

"I'll pray about it. In the meantime, do you have any cookies to go along with your fantastic iced tea?" Mar-tha asked, feeling pleased with her ability to remain calm through their whole discussion. Two weeks ago, she couldn't have kept from shedding tears. Maybe life would go on.

Chapter Twenty-Five

It was decided. Instead of meeting for the first time in a public restaurant, Lizzy agreed to offer her home for the reunion between Rose and Martha. When her niece first approached her about the idea, Lizzy was apprehensive, but as she and Martha talked it over, she decided it would be the best solution. Sarah never came by unannounced, and especially now since she depended on others to transport her. She never had enjoyed driving a horse and Melvin seemed happy to take over that task. Sarah would never have to learn of the meeting, though Lizzy wondered if her sister would really be that upset, since so many years had passed.

It would be easy for Rose to find Lizzy's home as well. All in all, it seemed like the right place for the two to have their first meeting. Lizzy didn't tell anyone else in the family. Only her husband knew about it, and he made plans to be at one of his brothers for the day.

As the time drew closer, Martha began to question her decision to meet with her birth mother. Would it stir up unresolved feelings? It was too late to change her mind though, and so she made an excuse ahead of time to be out of the house by ten in the morning. Since it was market day, it was easy to use that as a reason. She also told her parents she would like to take the whole day and shop for a few personal items. She didn't mention it until several days before the meeting would transpire. Her mother showed no signs of curiosity and merely asked her to pick up some granulated sugar while she was out.

The only glitch was when her grandmother suggested going with her to market. Martha certainly didn't want to hurt her feelings by refusing, but she mentioned being out all day and suggested *Dawdi* would miss her too much. That seemed to satisfy her and she decided to stay home and work on her mending. She considered quilting, but preferred to work with others on such a large project.

The day before the event was to take place, Martha was outside picking strawberries when she heard an auto come up the drive. She turned and watched as it stopped and a man stepped out of the passenger side. An Amishman. *Paul!* She nearly fainted. She could feel her heart palpitating wildly in her chest and actually had trouble drawing a breath. Her mother had gone in to work on the bread and her father was out in the field somewhere with his team of horses, which meant they'd be alone.

Martha stood motionless, watching as if she were observing actors in a play. Paul talked a moment with the driver and then removed a small satchel from the back seat and closed the car door. He walked slowly over to where Martha stood frozen in place. She was expressionless.

"Martha? Are you okay?" he asked, questioning with his blue eyes.

"*Jah*, maybe." She still didn't move.

"I'm sorry if I shocked you. I should have written I guess, but I didn't know what to say."

"I guess not."

He put the satchel down and held out his hands. She ignored them and remained in the same spot.

"I guess you're still mad."

"*Jah*, I guess so."

He laughed awkwardly. "Can we at least shake hands?"

She extended her right hand and waited for him to reach for it. He shook it once and then continued to hold her hand until she withdrew it.

"Why did you come?" she finally asked.

"You must know why. Because I don't want to fight with you anymore."

"We're not fighting. We're not doing anything."

"I know, but we need to get all this behind us."

"I don't know if I can."

"Do you want to?"

"I don't know. Maybe not."

"Martha, Martha. I can't go on like this. We need to at least talk about what happened."

"*Nee*. I don't have anything to say to you. I wish you hadn't come."

"I can't believe you mean that."

"I do."

"But, Martha, we loved each other so much and—"

"Loved. Once loved."

"Please let's go somewhere where we can talk."

"I don't know."

"I came all this way—"

"You shouldn't have. You should have written."

"I just thought it would be better to see each other."

"You were wrong."

"Honey, I'm so sorry I hurt you so bad. Please forgive me." He moved closer and placed his hands on her stiffened arms.

"Don't. Please don't touch me."

"I still love you, Martha."

"I'm sorry."

"You won't go somewhere and talk to me alone?"

"I can't."

"Or won't?"

"Same thing. Not yet. I can't take a chance and get hurt again. I'm finally healing. You'll have to leave."

"My ride left. Can I stay in your barn till you agree to talk?"

"It may never happen."

"I can't believe you won't even listen to me."

"I listened. I heard. There's nothing more to say."

"It's Daniel, isn't it? He's back in your life and you think you love him."

"No. No one is my life right now, and I like it this way."

They stood facing each other. No tears were shed. Their voices remained calm. No animosity displayed. Just two young people, who had once planned to live their lives together, staring at each other—almost as strangers.

After a full two or three minutes, Paul turned and headed for the road. She watched as he removed his cell phone to make a call. It was probably his driver. He couldn't have gotten too far. She continued to watch the man she still loved, as he walked down the road towards the highway. He didn't look back. Right or wrong, she had sealed their fate. There would be no marriage. There would be no reconciliation. The moment he disappeared from sight, she fell to her knees and wailed like an animal. The sounds barely penetrated her mind. It was someone else in charge of her brain. She felt totally unable to think rationally. And it hurt. Terrible-bad.

Paul was silent for the entire trip back. He even sat in the back seat so he wouldn't have to converse. Since his driver had had to turn around only fifteen minutes after leaving him off, he didn't expect Paul to be in a good mood.

Martha seemed so different from the sweet happy girl he knew so well. He'd truly broken her heart by his moment of weakness. Oh, if he could live it over again. Things would be so different. It was shocking to realize he could be swayed so easily into responding to a woman's trickery. Were all men that weak? Dear, beautiful Martha. What had he done to her? Even her eyes showed her deep pain. Pain he'd caused. He wasn't worth her. She was an honorable woman. He would trust her in any situation to be loyal. But hopefully, she wouldn't rebound and fall for the likes of that Daniel guy. He could see right through him. He was as phony as they came, but some men were as convincing as Hazel had been with him. What a fool. That's what he'd been. A blind fool. Jeremiah could be in for a terrible marriage. Paul hoped she'd be totally faithful to his friend if they did marry.

It would be embarrassing to show up back at the shop

today after saying he'd be gone for two nights. What on earth made him so conceited as to think he'd be welcomed with open arms after what he'd put her through?

He pictured her taking care of her mother. She'd be so kind to her—bathing her, holding her head when she was sick, feeding her special meals she'd be able to tolerate. Of course, she was needed at home. Her father was far too busy farming to be much of a nurse to his wife. Besides, most likely, a woman needs her daughter at a time like this.

Paul certainly hadn't made it easy on Martha, demanding she leave everything behind to be with him. How unfair to dangle the home, as well as an established business, in front of her eyes to tempt her to leave her family behind at this crucial time. Even if he was fortunate enough to end up with her as his bride, she'd have to endure living as a close neighbor to a woman she knew had tried to seduce her husband. A woman, who had nearly gotten her way with such a weak man, just through her kiss and her bold ways. No proper Amish girl would flaunt her beauty the way Hazel had, by releasing her golden tresses to tempt a man not her husband. It would have been acceptable only if they'd truly planned to marry and even then, it was questionable.

Could he put Martha through the humiliation of having to be friends with Hazel?

What if he talked it over with Jeremiah and asked to be released of his contract in the business? It seemed Jeremiah had considered breaking their agreement when he was upset. Now the shoe was on the other foot, and it might not be that difficult to alter their plans. Ben would stay on and he was a valuable worker.

If Paul couldn't get a job working for a furniture

maker in Paradise or nearby, he could start out all over. Until his income was sufficient to provide for him and his bride, he could rent a room somewhere nearby—if he'd be fortunate enough to convince her to marry him. It would be nice to be near her family. Lancaster was a beautiful county. The land was amazing—fertile and lush. Martha would be near her grandparents as well. Even though her bishop was stricter than his, he could deal with that. For heaven's sake, he could deal with anything! If he had Martha by his side.

Calm settled in as he pictured this new plan. It could make all the difference in the world to Martha. He had been thinking only of himself. It came as a shock to realize he'd been selfish when planning their future. Even if her mother recovered completely from her bout with cancer, Martha and she were very close. Probably closer than most mothers and daughters, perhaps because Martha was chosen and not just the result of a biological happening. There was something special between them, and it dawned on him that he might have been jealous in some way. He tried to reject the thought, but it smashed right back into his mind. *Oh,* Gott, *I've been so blind. Forgive me.*

The ride was finally over and he paid his driver a block from the property. Then he walked around the outer perimeter of their land so he wouldn't be seen by Jeremiah or Ben, and made his way to the back door of his home. Instead of working the rest of the day, he spent the time reading his Bible and praying aloud. Another area of his life he'd let slip. If he was to be the spiritual leader of his home, he needed to put himself aside and gain his strength and wisdom from his Creator. This was a good beginning.

Chapter Twenty-Six

There was no time to indulge in self-pity. Martha needed to prepare mentally for the next day when she'd be meeting with her birth mother. Why had she agreed to meet this woman after all these years? It would be awkward, at best. And what was there really to say? If healing needed to take place, it would be for Rose. She had been the one to suffer. After all, Martha didn't even know about the adoption until recently, and her childhood had been ideal. She always felt secure in her parents' love for her. Though her father tended to be stricter than her mother, she knew it was done out of love and the desire to make her a better person in the end. She'd been a compliant child and therefore, there were very few times when she needed to be disciplined.

She remembered once when she had lied about doing one of her chores. She just hadn't felt like feeding the chickens one morning and wanted to play hop-scotch instead, but the poor hungry fowl had created quite a stir, which made her father suspicious of the reason for their dilemma, and after Martha confessed, she was scolded and sent to her room for the rest of the day.

There were probably other times, though none stood out in her mind.

There were times where she'd been lonely and wished for brothers and sisters like so many of her school friends had. As she grew older, her mother explained she wasn't able to have more children, and the ties between Martha and her mother grew even stronger.

Though Rose Esh was just a name to Martha, perhaps it would be good to learn more about her life, and she might even learn more about herself, since some of the blanks would be filled in. It was strange, but Martha was actually more curious about her father. Perhaps, since she resembled him more physically, she felt drawn to him on a subconscious level.

Aside from prayer, there was little she could do for preparation. She did spend extra time shampooing her hair, though there was not much exposed, once the *kapp* was added. She also trimmed her nails and tried to brush under them and remove the traces of dirt from all her weeding. Her grandmother used to tease her when she'd come in from playing with dirt wedged under her nails. "Looks like your nails are in mourning," she'd say.

The surprise visit from Paul had been filed in a "do not touch" area of her brain for another time. She simply couldn't handle any more emotional crises in the forefront of her fragile mind at this point. Her mother's health was never far from her thoughts, and though she felt things would work out in the end, she never lost the dark shadow that loomed over her night and day that the cancer might have advanced too far to be cured.

* * *

The next morning arrived as every other morning. The dawn was announced by their faithful rooster, and then she heard the familiar steps of her parents as they proceeded to start their day with a hearty meal. Her father usually tended to some of his farm chores while her mother fried up homemade sausage or scrapple in the black iron pan. Nothing seemed out of place this morning, though Martha's hand shook as she twisted her hair into a bun and pushed the hairpins in place, taking slightly more time to make it tidy. It wouldn't do to look sloppy for her introduction to Rose. It would reflect badly on her upbringing. She slipped one of her newer frocks on—a green cotton, which fit her nicely. Her hands felt awkward as she pinned the closure on her neckline and then added her matching apron. Without a decent size mirror, she was unable to view herself as she'd be seen by her mother. Her sneakers were rather old and needed to be replaced, but they were comfortable and at least, not threadbare.

The morning seemed to drag as she kneaded the bread and then set it aside to rise. She considered taking a few of her molasses cookies for Rose, but feared her mother might notice and questions would arise.

Finally, it was time to leave for her aunt's. Her mother was sitting on the back porch, knitting a sweater for a neighbor's unborn child. She looked up as Martha opened the screen door and stepped onto the porch. "Don't forget the sugar. Five pounds will be enough. You can take money from the jar above the refrigerator."

"It's okay. I'm happy to use my money. I still feel guilty that you won't take anything for my room and board."

"Oh mercy, child, we do just fine. You need to save your money for your future."

"Whatever that may be," Martha added, under her breath.

"What was that, Martha? I couldn't hear you."

"It was nothing, *Mamm*. I'll see you later." She leaned down to kiss her mother's soft cheek. She always smelled the same. A lovely lavender scent. It was one of her mother's admitted luxuries. She purchased lavender soap from the grocer, even though it was a dollar more for three bars.

Melvin helped his daughter set up the buggy and handed her the reins. "Now you have a nice time, Martha. Take your time. We'll do just fine till you get back."

"*Danki*. I started a roast for your dinner. *Mamm* said she'd handle the rest."

"It's *gut* for her to work in the kitchen. Makes her feel almost normal."

"*Jah*, I know. You still have hope she'll be cured, don't you?" she asked.

"Of course. I don't think of it any other way. She's strong and she seems to be doing real gut, don't you think?"

"I do, *Daed*. I'm very hopeful."

Martha directed the horse over to the drive and made her way over to her aunt's house, arriving about a half hour before Rose was to show up. Now that the time had actually arrived, she was less apprehensive and even excited at the thought of meeting the woman who had given birth to her.

When she walked into the kitchen, Lizzy was icing a cake. It was a yellow cake with thick chocolate frosting. When Martha was a young girl, she'd always ask her aunt if she had any *chalko* cake, and nine times out of ten, she had at least one generous-size piece waiting for the little dark-eyed beauty.

Martha went over and dipped her forefinger into the bowl with the remaining icing.

"Still your favorite?" her aunt asked, as she set the spatula off to the side.

"*Jah*, when you make it," she said, licking her finger while closing her eyes. Then she leaned over and embraced her aunt.

"Ready to meet Rose?" Lizzy asked.

Martha withdrew and let out a long breath. "As ready as I'll ever be. I'm kinda nervous."

"Well, believe it or not, so am I," Lizzy said.

"Will you help me end it, if it doesn't go *gut*?" Martha asked.

"You mean, push her out the door or something?"

Martha giggled. "I was thinking more of mentioning we had plans for later or something a little kinder."

"You know I won't lie, Martha, but I'll try to think of something if I see you're getting upset. I don't think she plans to spend much time here. But surely you don't want me to stick around the whole time."

"Oh, but I do! It's going to be so awkward. I don't know what we'll find to talk about."

"She probably just wants to get to know you a little."

"I think she still feels guilty, by the way the letters read."

"I barely remember the girl. I just recall she hardly spoke, and the poor thing cried through most of the visit. It was hard on everyone."

"But you said I seemed to bond with my *mamm* right away."

"Oh *jah*. You didn't cry at all when she held you. It was almost as if you knew she'd be your *mudder*."

There was a rap on the front door and Lizzy started to move toward the front, but stopped. "Why don't you answer it, Martha?"

"Me?"

"*Jah*, of course. Go now."

Martha felt perspiration forming under her arms and on her forehead. Goodness.

When she opened the door, Rose was standing with a small bouquet of spring flowers, looking every bit as nervous as Martha felt.

"Come in, please." Martha smiled as sweetly as she could. Rose handed her the flowers and smiled.

"*Danki*. I'll put them in water." She was impressed with the woman's gentle deep blue eyes. She was fairly short and quite slender. Pretty looking, though not beautiful. She had delicate features and pale skin. Her blonde hair was short and looked quite fashionably styled.

Rose looked around while they stood in the vestibule. "It's a nice house. Old?"

"I don't know," Martha said. "We can ask my aunt. She's in the kitchen. Want to go there or in the living room?"

"Wherever you'd like me," Rose said.

"Okay, I like kitchens the best. I feel they're more homey."

"Oh, I agree," Rose said, smiling broadly. "I spend a lot of time in my own kitchen, though I don't cook much for myself, since I live alone."

"I see."

Lizzy went right over to greet her and she shook her hand. "It's been a long time."

"Yes, twenty years. You look the same."

"You don't," Lizzy said kiddingly. "You sure were young then."

"Too young to find myself in that predicament."

"Here, sit," Lizzy said, pointing to one of the pine kitchen chairs. "I just finished icing a cake. Would you like a piece with some fresh *kaffi*?"

"That would be real nice. The cake looks delicious."

"It's Martha's favorite. Even now. Right, Martha?"

"*Jah*. Even now," she repeated. They sat across from each other while Lizzy cut three pieces and laid them on the table. She'd placed her favorite tablecloth on for the occasion, which had a white center with a deep border of bright red cherries. Martha recognized it from her early childhood.

"Cute cloth," Rose said as she moved her hand over the plain center.

"*Danki*. Martha always loved it, didn't you, honey?"

"*Jah*, I haven't seen it for years."

"Do you take cream in your *kaffi*?" Lizzy asked her guest.

"I like it black, thank you."

The three women sat and sipped their coffees, as an awkward silence prevailed for several minutes.

"So, Martha tells me you write books," Lizzy finally remarked.

"Yes, and I'm just starting a new one."

"About the Amish?" Martha asked.

"No, this one is about the Revolutionary War. The characters are fictional, but I set it during the war since many of my readers like my books based on history."

"That must be hard," Martha stated, as she cut into her cake, which for some reason, had no taste.

"Actually, I like to do the research." The conversation continued for several minutes centered on how her research was done and she spoke of some of the places she'd visited related to the war. "I'm probably going to spend a few days checking out some of the battleground sites here in Pennsylvania."

"*Jah*, I went to the Brandywine battlefield one time. I liked the bus ride the best," Martha said, smiling over.

Rose laughed gently. "Oh, all children love to ride buses—and trains."

They each sipped their coffee at the same time.

"Tell me how your parents are doing?" Lizzy asked, unable to think of anything more exciting to talk about.

"I heard from my sister recently that my father had died a while back, however I haven't kept in touch with anyone else in my family. I left Ohio soon after everything happened."

"Oh, I'm sorry about your father," Lizzy said, as she pushed the last piece of cake from one side of her plate to the other.

"Thank you, but it's okay. Apparently, his heart gave him problems for years. My mother is still alive, though we don't communicate. I hope to one day. Maybe we can even talk on the phone sometime." She turned to Martha. "Tell me about yourself. What do you like to do the most? Do you like to sing?"

"Oh, *jah*. Very much. *Mamm* and I often sing together as we work. And I love to sing at church service." This opened up a whole new area for discussion and Rose told about joining a local chorus. They even mentioned knowing some of the same hymns.

Lizzy sat back and watched their exchange, pleased with the way Martha was handling things.

After nearly an hour of catching up on Martha's early years and Rose sharing some of her life experiences, they walked out in the yard together and Lizzy showed off her flower gardens.

"They're beautiful, Liz. You have a real talent," Rose said. Then she stopped walking and looked over at Martha. "I hope things are better now with your young man."

"Actually, they're worse. It's over, I'm afraid."

"That's a shame," Rose said, her eyes showing her concern.

"I think he'll come around and give you a call or something," Lizzy remarked.

"He came by yesterday."

"Really? Well, how about that." Lizzy patted Martha's arm. "Come, let us sit under the tree." They walked over and sat on some folding chairs in the shade. Lizzy continued the conversation. "And did he apologize?"

"Kind of, but I didn't want to talk to him."

"I'm surprised he didn't stay overnight."

"He wanted to, but I told him no. I'm just going through too much with *Mamm* and all right now. I can't deal with anything else."

Rose looked concerned. "Is there anything wrong with your mother?"

Lizzy answered. "My sister is battling cancer. She's been on chemo, and she gets sick sometimes from it."

"Oh dear, I sure picked a bad time to visit, didn't I?"

"It's okay," Martha said. "It can't be helped."

Lizzy continued. "Martha had her own apartment and a job before Sarah got sick. She came home to take care of her."

"That's so good of you, Martha."

"Well, she's my *mudder*. I mean…well, she needed me."

"How is she doing now?" Rose asked.

"We'll know more next month. They'll probably do a CT scan to check. We're very hopeful." Martha looked away and smoothed down her apron.

"Would it be better if I come back at another time?" Rose asked.

Martha shook her head. "It's fine. You came all the way out to meet me. I appreciate that."

Rose smiled. "I had hoped I'd find a happier young lady."

"Oh, if you're thinking I haven't been happy, you're wrong. I've had a wonderful-*gut* life so far. My parents have done everything possible to give me a *gut* life. And I not only had them growing up, but I had my aunt here and her husband and her kids and their kids. Please don't get the wrong idea."

Rose's eyes filled. "You misunderstood me. I meant because of that young man causing you pain. I'm so glad about your happy childhood, Martha. You'll never know. Not a day has gone by that I haven't thought of my beautiful baby girl. If I'd only been older…or my parents had been more open…well, I would have raised you myself. But I see I made the right decision in the end."

"*Jah*, you made the only one you could, I think," Martha said. "I'm glad you had me adopted by Amish people, too. I've been part of the English world for a time, and though I met some wonderful people, I much prefer the way we live. I'm sorry you left the Amish."

"At the time, it seemed like the only thing I could do to find happiness of any kind. My parents couldn't forgive me for the disgrace I'd brought them. Things were never the same for me at home."

"Have you found happiness?" Martha asked softly, looking into her eyes.

"Contentment is a better word. I was married for a time to a real nice man. I think I loved him, but if you couldn't call it love, it was still special. He treated me well, and we had some good years. Now that I'm alone, I get pleasure in my writing. I'm a strong believer, and God has brought me through my trials. My church family is always there for me as well, and I also have several close friends. It could be a lot worse."

Lizzy sat quietly watching as the two shared their thoughts with each other.

"Maybe someday you'll marry again," Martha said.

"Perhaps, though I don't need marriage the way some people do."

"I think I'm the same way," Martha said.

Lizzy rolled her eyes. "You're kidding, Martha. You've talked of nothing else since you were ten years old. I'm a bit shocked that you made Paul go back home without talking things over with him."

"If he really loves you, Martha," Rose said, "he'll be back. He'd be a fool to let you go."

"Maybe he'd be better off without me."

"I don't believe that for a second. Even though we've only just met, I know in my heart, you're a good person. I read it in your eyes and your words."

Martha smiled. "I'm glad you came to see me."

"So am I."

"Can I ask you something?" Martha said.

"Anything."

"What about my father? Do you ever hear from him?"

"No. It turns out he wrote to me many times after he left America, but my parents hid the letters from me. I found out from my sister about the letters. He never knew about you."

"If he'd known, do you think he would have come back to America?"

"I have no way of knowing. About five years ago, I read about an Italian man with his name who had started a business in New York City. He had a chain of art galleries featuring Italian artists. I don't know if it was him, since it's a fairly common name."

"Was there a picture of him in the article?"

"Yes, but it was small and I couldn't really tell much. It was too difficult to make out his features. I doubt it was him, but I was tempted to write. I just never did."

"I asked, because I kind of identify with the Italian side of my heritage. After all, I look a lot like him."

"How would you know that?" she asked.

"I have a picture."

"Oh, that's right. You mentioned that in your letter. That's more than I have. How did you get it?"

"I gave it to her," Lizzy said, breaking in. "Martha, do you have it with you?"

"No, it's at home. It's in the drawer with your letters," she said, looking over at Rose.

"I guess your mother, your other mother, doesn't know about today."

"No, I'm afraid she'd be upset."

Rose nodded. "I guess I can understand, though I'm certainly not a threat. I have no illusions about our relationship, Martha. Sarah is the one who raised you, took care of you when you were sick, dressed you and protected you. That makes her the real mother. I just need to ask…have you forgiven me?"

The question came so rapidly, Martha sat back before answering. "There is nothing to forgive, in fact just the opposite. I should thank you for putting my needs ahead of your own desires. It must have been a difficult decision to make, especially since I know what a kind person you are."

"It was definitely the worst day of my life when I parted with you, but seeing the woman you've become, I know it was the right decision. And it may end the nightmares I've had over the years, wondering if I'd been wrong to let you go. Sarah and Melvin did a wonderful job of raising you. I'll be eternally grateful, and someday I hope to be able to talk to them about it. I need to thank them."

Lizzy smiled over. "That day may come. Once my sister is cured, I'll have a talk with her. I didn't like to be secretive about this meeting, but I'm sure you understand."

"Oh, I do. Of course." She turned to Martha. "I'm going to leave you now, but please, let's stay in touch by letters. I sent you my phone number in case you have an opportunity to call. I will pray for you and your Paul. It sounds as if you two will one day reconcile."

"Maybe. I have to confess I still love him, but he's hurt me badly."

"Martha, you have forgiven me. Surely whatever it is that happened between you two can't be as serious as what happened with us. Let God soften your heart. Forgive him and move on with your life. It's the only way to live."

Martha nodded, her lips trembling. Then she and Rose walked around to the front where Rose had parked the car. Lizzy stayed back and remained seated to allow them time to themselves.

Rose turned to Martha. Her cheeks were moist. She stretched out her arms and her beautiful baby girl accepted her embrace. They remained together for several minutes, sharing tears, but no words.

Their memory would last a lifetime.

Chapter Twenty-Seven

July was a scorcher. The Troyer generator, which was powered by their tall windmill, worked constantly to keep the fans running throughout the house. Sarah was nearly through with her week of chemo. Her vomiting had ceased after the second dose thanks to the medication she received. Her spirits were good, knowing these might be the last of the chemotherapy treatments.

It was only at night sometimes, when she lay in bed next to Melvin that she would consider the alternatives to a healing. Death didn't frighten her. She loved the Lord with all her heart and though she didn't hear it through her church, she read enough of the Bible to believe that it wasn't through works one was saved, but through the death and resurrection of her Lord. Through His grace and unconditional love, and her solid faith and full commitment to Him she would live eternally in His kingdom. Whatever sins she had committed in her life, or would commit in the future, had already been paid for with His precious blood. She truly believed she'd end up in Paradise with Him someday. She smiled in the darkness. Paradise. Here she was living in Paradise,

Pennsylvania. *I won't even have to change my address. Only my frail body.*

In spite of her confidence, she dreaded the thought of leaving her loved ones behind to grieve. Melvin, especially. He counted on her for everything. In fact, he could barely find anything on his own in the house. He'd ask her when he needed scissors, or Scotch tape, or just about anything. "They're where they've been for nineteen years," she'd say. "You'd better learn, Melvin, for Pete's sake."

Perhaps, he didn't want to learn. Maybe it was his way of holding on to her.

Oh, Lord, if it be Your will, please give me more time on this earth to care for my dear husband. And for my sweet Martha. I also pray, Father, that You will bring Paul back to her. I see how she grieves for him. And help me to be more independent so she will be free to move with Paul if they marry. I have been selfish, expecting her to live her life to please me. I'm so sorry. Forgive me. And whatever happens, Father, I accept it as Your will. I love You and I think I'll sleep now. Danki."

She snuggled closer to Melvin, who was snoring rhythmically and almost inaudibly, and soon fell into a peaceful sleep.

On Wednesday, Martha made her way to the open market to do some shopping. She looked forward to this time, and usually treated herself to a light lunch at the local diner. Today, she decided to just head over to the ice cream parlor where she'd received the letter from her birth mother. Unfortunately, the waitress who had helped to bring them together was off for the day, but Martha decided to order an ice cream sundae anyway.

As she reached the last few spoonsful, a couple came through the front door and took a table on the other side of the room. The man looked familiar. Lo and behold, it was Daniel! He certainly didn't look Amish anymore. His hair was stylishly short, and his dress was more English than Amish. He wore jeans and a shirt with the name of a football team. The girl was definitely English. She had on jeans also, though it looked as if she was poured into them, they were so tight. Her top was open under her bra, exposing her stomach—even her belly button!

After ordering, Daniel looked over for the first time. His mouth dropped open and he nodded. Then he leaned over and whispered in the girl's ear. She shrugged as he stood and went over to Martha's table. "Hey, how are you doing?" he asked casually.

"I'm *gut*. I guess I know why you haven't been around," she added, looking across at the girl, who was tapping messages on her cell phone.

"Oh, her. Well, I've been painting and stuff at her house. We just thought we'd go out for some ice cream to cool off. How's your *mamm*?"

"On her last week of chemo, thank goodness."

"And you, Martha? How are you doing? Still going with Paul?"

"Mmm. I'm doing just wonderful-*gut*, *danki*."

"I'm glad. Well, I see our sundaes are coming over. I'd better go. Say hi to your family. I'll try to stop by when things get less busy."

"Daniel, I'm glad you've found someone else. I believe you realize it would never have worked for us."

His face reddened and he cleared his throat. "I really cared about you, Martha, but I'm afraid that whole Amish thing was a farce for me. If I couldn't have you, there was no point in dealing with all the dumb rules. I'm much happier now that I'm free. I guess I was living a lie."

"Being Amish is a real commitment. One I don't mind making, but you never seemed quite content, even when you tried."

"And I did try. I really did."

"Danny, your ice cream is melting," the girl called over.

"I guess I'd better go. I hope you and Paul will be very happy, Martha. You're quite a girl."

"Danki," she said, raising her hand for a handshake. He took it and covered her hand with his other left hand.

"Be good."

"I'll try," she said, smiling. When he left, she tucked a dollar for a tip under her dish and paid at the register. She didn't look over again until she got to the door. She turned to wave, but he was eating his ice cream with one hand and holding the girl's hand with his other. His attention was totally on his date.

Her relief was nearly palpable. She needn't worry about upsetting him anymore. He looked happy and this time it didn't seem phony. Her instincts had been right. A marriage with Daniel would have been a disaster.

Paul checked his mailbox before heading back to his house for the evening. Only one piece of mail was waiting for him. An advertisement for hearing aids.

He tossed it in the trash and made himself a salad for supper. As he sat alone in the house he intended for his bride-to-be, he thought over his potential future. When he and Jeremiah discussed the possibility of breaking the contract, his partner had said it would be fine with him, but he suggested Paul go slowly. He felt there was no point in giving up his business and the house if it was over between him and Martha.

"You'd better check with Martha first, and see if she's still interested in you. I don't mean to put a damper on things, but what you told me happened when you drove all the way to her home, makes me wonder if you're being realistic. She wouldn't even give you a chance to apologize. She may mean it when she says it's over. Don't complicate your life even more by jumping too quickly."

When he thought it over, it made perfect sense. He had to get her to listen to him so he could explain, but he wouldn't try to surprise her again. She'd have to agree ahead of time to meet with him.

Why hadn't he written to her sooner, instead of waiting for her to write first? It sure wasn't going to happen. She'd made that clear.

Paul reached for a writing pad and a pen and tried to write. He thought he'd apologized enough. He could run through the whole thing again, hoping she'd read it and accept it as truth, but instead of reiterating the same old message, he merely wrote,

"I love you with all my heart. I want you to be my wife. Please give me another chance."

Then he folded it up and addressed the envelope. If that didn't work, he'd send another note in a few days. Maybe he'd just have to wear her out, before she'd relent and let him come in person.

After washing the bowl from his salad, he placed it

in the drying rack and made his way over to the sofa. He picked up his Bible and raised the wick on his kerosene lamp. He'd read through the gospels and now he was halfway through the Book of Acts.

Before going to bed, he prayed, asking God for guidance, and if he and Martha were not meant to be together, he asked God to give him peace. God would have to perform a miracle to do that, he thought, as he laid his head on his pillow and attempted to sleep.

Sarah sat on a stool next to their bed as Melvin rubbed her shoulders and neck. "I guess I did too much today. Martha told me to stop scrubbing the floor, but it felt *gut*, you know what I mean?"

"Sure. You just want to live normal-like, but right now, you need to rest up, Sarah. Does this help?" he added a little coconut oil to his hands and rubbed more into her neck.

"Oh *jah*. It feels *gut. Danki*."

"Anytime."

"I have to talk to you about something, Melvin. I hope you're not too tired to listen."

"I'm fine. What is it?"

"It's about Martha. And the cell phone we took from her."

"Oh, that again."

"Well, I haven't talked about it in a long time, but you see how she is. She looks so unhappy."

"Well, a phone ain't going to make any difference."

"I think it would. If she could call and talk to Paul…"

"I think she's over that young man."

"*Nee.* I don't think she'll ever be over him. You look

at her eyes, Melvin. She has rings as dark as midnight under them."

"What's that got to do with a cell phone?"

"It's because she doesn't sleep *gut*. She admitted it. She's up half the night."

"What for?"

"*Ach*, don't men know anything? She's still in love with Paul, and she's plain miserable without him."

"Okay, and the phone?"

"If she had the phone, she could talk to him and they could get things ironed out."

"She wouldn't even talk to him when he came in person. What makes you think it would work out over the phone."

"Well, maybe it wouldn't, but it could."

"I thought you didn't want her to marry Paul. You acted like it would be the end of the world if she moved away."

"I've changed. I realize now it was selfish of me to act that way. Love doesn't come around all that often. They had something special, and I sure don't want to be a reason for them to be apart."

"If it means that much to you—"

"It does, honey. *Danki!*" she turned and put her chin up for a kiss.

"Now, I didn't say it was okay…"

"Oh, but that's what you meant. I'll give it to her tomorrow. She'll have to get it charged up somehow."

"You know all about those things."

"That's about all I know."

"Well, it's more than I do. All right, honey, just don't go talkin' about it to people."

"You're the best, and you can stop massaging my neck now. It feels much better."

"Okay, but I wouldn't mind another of those sweet kisses you were giving out."

Sarah moved over to the bed. He followed her over and sat close to her. She gave him a tender pat on the cheek and then kissed him soundly on the lips. It was wonderful to be close to her dear husband, and for once, her nausea was completely gone.

Chapter Twenty-Eight

Martha was not as thrilled about being allowed to use her cell phone as her parents had anticipated. She took it, after thanking them, and placed it in her bureau drawer, next to the picture of her father and the letters she'd received from Rose. A second phone sat in the back of the same drawer.

Two days later, it was market day again. After much deliberation, she decided to get the phone charged up, whether she'd actually use it or not. She placed the phone in her pocket along with some money, and made her way into town. The only place she could think of to charge it was the public library, so before buying her groceries, she walked over to the library and asked permission to use one of their outlets.

The librarian was very nice about it and showed her where she could plug it in. While she waited, Martha looked along the rows of Amish books. She couldn't remember Rose's pen name, so she checked the pictures of the authors on the backs of each book. Finally, after nearly half an hour, she found one of the books her birth mother had written.

While she waited for the charge to be completed, she began reading one of the books. It was dedicated to "a family who opened up their home and hearts to a needy child. May God put His blessings upon their home and their lives."

She realized who it was intended for, and it brought a sweet feeling to her heart.

The book was about a young woman who was in love with a Mennonite. It was quite interesting, so she filled out some paperwork and they issued her a library card so she could check out the book at home.

Once the phone charge was over ninety percent, she removed it, tucked it in her pocket and headed to the marketplace, where she bought a few items for home. The pineapples were at a reasonable price, so she added one to her order.

When she arrived home, her mother greeted her with a letter addressed to her. "I thought you'd want to read this right away." Paul's name and address were printed neatly in the left-hand corner.

Martha thanked her and after putting away some of the groceries, she went outside and sat under her favorite maple tree. It certainly couldn't have taken him long to write the message. At first it annoyed her that he hadn't written more, but then she read it over. And over. It touched her heart, probably more than a five-page missile would have, under the circumstances. Should she call him? If so, when? While he was working? *Nee*, that would not be wise. If she decided to call, it should be in the evening when he was free, though apparently, he was used to putting in long hours. And what if a female voice answered? Then it would be over! *Again*.

She looked at the phone and contemplated her choices. Maybe she wouldn't call at all.

Sarah was lugging the laundry basket out the kitchen door when Martha spotted her. "Wait, *Mamm*. Let me get it. You know *Daed* would have a fit to see you lifting that." She walked quickly over, as her mother stood up straight and smiled.

"I'd better get used to working on my own."

"I'm usually here, *Mamm*. Just wait for me."

"Well, we need to talk about that, Martha. Help me with these towels and then we can sit together and chat."

Martha looked at her curiously. "I made lemonade before I left this morning. I can get us a pitcher, if you'd like."

"That would be nice. Let's get these towels hanging first. Oh, it's another hot one."

"*Jah*, for sure," Martha said as she carried the wicker basket out to the clothesline. They hummed a favorite hymn as they pinned the towels in the sun. Then Martha went in to get the lemonade and glasses. She brought out extra ones. "I thought maybe we'd get *Mammi* and *Dawdi* to join us," Martha said.

"*Jah*, but not just yet. I want to talk about something important first."

They took their seats and Martha poured them each a glass of the cool liquid and placed the pitcher back on the picnic table.

"I'm sure Paul is still trying to win your heart back, or he wouldn't be writing to you, and from the way you act when his name comes up, I know you still care for him. I would guess you're still in love with each other, though maybe your pride is holding you back—"

"*Mamm*, you—"

"Hush. Let me speak."

"Sorry," Martha said, chagrined.

"I have done a lot of praying and thinking, and I realize I've been putting myself ahead of everyone else. I see you shaking your head, but just hear me out. The way I see it, I'm using the cancer to get my way about things. Here you've met a fine young Amishman, who is very ambitious and wants to provide well for his family. He's put his own feelings aside to make a *gut* living and he seems like an honorable young man. I know, he made a mistake. A big one. And I know you were hurt real bad, but he's asked for forgiveness. He's promised it won't happen again, and I for one, believe he means it.

"Now, this is important, Martha. If you marry Paul, you need to move to the home he's providing for you. He has a business, and so it's important for you to support him and make a nice home for him. Your *daed* and me will be just fine. We can visit you as often as you'd like us to, since your *daed* has set aside enough money for our future. I will not be, and should not be, an issue for you. You are going to lead your own life. That's it. I'm done." Sarah sat back and folded her arms.

Martha stared at her and then went over and knelt beside her. "You're the most amazing *mudder* in the whole world. With all you're going through—you're worried about me. How on earth could I leave you?"

"You would, because I'm telling you to. You have to obey me. And I've thought it through, and this is what I believe. Distance can't remove our love for each other, Martha. You will always be my wonderful *dochder*, but I'm looking beyond the cancer, and I know this is the right thing to do, regardless of whether I get healed or not. Please, don't argue with me. Let me be the person *Gott* wants me to be."

"Oh, Mamm." Martha let her tears flow. "I will listen to you, as I always have, because you're way wiser than I am. I've decided to call Paul tonight and have him come out again—if he still cares. I'll tell him what you've said, but only if things go right between us."

"*Jah*, that's *gut*. You call him and don't let him hang up on you."

"He'd better not! That would not be *schmaert* of him!"

Sarah laughed. "Oh, I don't think he'd do anything like that. I was kidding you."

"I know," Martha said, grinning through her tears. "I love you."

"I know, and I love you, bushels and bushels."

"And more than the grains of sand."

"*Jah* for sure."

Chapter Twenty-Nine

Paul was ready to turn in for the night. Even though it was only eight-thirty, his evenings dragged. He could have gone to visit Eb and Deborah, but he didn't have the energy, and he always feared he'd run into Hazel.

His phone rang and he answered it without checking the caller ID. When a woman's voice responded to his greeting, he recognized Martha's voice immediately.

"Martha, is it really you?"

"*Jah*, it's me. Surprised?"

He let out a quick laugh. "Very, and happy! Is everything okay?"

"*Nee*. Not at all."

"Oh no, is it your *mamm*?"

"No, Paul, I mean everything's not okay, because we've been fighting. You and me."

"But we aren't anymore, right?"

"It's up to you, I guess."

"I never want to argue with you—about anything."

"Do you want to come by and see me?"

"You'll talk to me this time?"

"*Jah*."

"And you'll listen with your heart, as well as your ears?"

"I think I can do that."

"When can I come?"

"Anytime."

"Tomorrow?"

He heard her familiar giggle. "If you want to."

"I'd come tonight, but I need to get Skip, my driver."

"*Jah*, tomorrow would be fine. I plan to be home all day. And you can stay with my *aenti*, if you want."

"You sure?"

"*Jah.*"

"Oh, Martha, my sweet—"

"Wait, Paul, we haven't made up yet. Things have to be straightened out first."

"You're right. Absolutely right! Okay, I'll try to get a ride first thing in the morning. In fact, I'll ride over to Skip's tonight since it's not late yet, and get my ride all set up. Just hope he's available."

"If you can't get here tomorrow, would you call me? I'll leave my phone on."

"Do your folks know you're using it?"

"*Jah*, they're permitting it."

"Wow! I can't believe it."

"There are lots of things you won't believe, but I'll wait till I see you."

"I hope I can sleep."

Martha giggled again. "Me, too. It's kinda scary."

"Don't be frightened, Martha. We can work anything out, with *Gott*'s help."

"*Jah*, if it be His will."

"I'll say good-bye now so I can get over to Skip's in the light."

"Okay. Good night, Paul."

"*Gut nacht.*" After hanging up, Paul got on his knees and thanked God, over and over. Then he quickly made his way over to Skip's house and set the ride up for eight the next morning. Wait till Martha heard he was willing to move to Paradise! That might make all the difference!

Before leaving for Paradise, Paul called Martha's phone to say he hoped to be at her place between ten and ten-thirty. Since she hadn't answered, he left the message.

Martha had turned off the ringer, but she checked his message after breakfast and felt her heart rate rise at the anticipation of seeing Paul again. This would be either a fantastic day, or one of her worst! Her mother seemed pleased that he was coming, and she made plans to work on the quilt in the *dawdi haus* to give the young couple more privacy to talk. Lizzy was scheduled to come by anyway. She and *Mammi* were determined to finish the quilt for Martha by the fall. Perhaps they knew something no one else did!

Martha paced the whole first floor. She changed her dress twice, finally settling on her navy blue one, since it was her newest. She was planning on baking off some cookies, but she was too nervous to concentrate on a recipe, though she could practically bake them in her sleep.

Finally, around quarter after ten, Skip's auto made the turn into their drive and slowly headed for the front of the house. She could have run out to meet him, but she didn't want to look too anxious, and she preferred not having an audience, just in case Paul wanted to give her a hug.

She watched from behind the sheer white curtain as Paul talked with the driver. Then he reached in the back seat for his satchel and headed towards the house. Her mother was already at the *dawdi haus*, along with *Aenti* Liz. Her father was out in the barn.

Paul walked around to the back door and knocked. She tried not to rush to open it, but the temptation was too strong and she took three long steps to reach the door handle. When she opened it, he stood a moment and grinned at her. "Hi."

"Hi, yourself. Come on in."

He walked in and placed his satchel on the floor by the door and extended his right hand for a shake. Goodness!

When she placed her hand in his, he pulled her gently towards him and then wrapped his arms around her, whispering her name over and over. "I've missed you so much."

"*Jah*, me, too," she responded, out of breath, as he squeezed her so tightly, she wondered if her eyes would bulge out!

When he released her, she put her hands on either side of her cheeks. "Wow!"

Laughing, he reached for her one hand and walked with her to the front room where they sat on the sofa, their legs just touching. "I guess we need to talk," he said, tilting his head.

"I guess we should."

"I'm afraid to say the wrong thing."

"I know. Let's take our time and not get upset with each other. I have something important to say, if we make up."

"I think we've already made up," he said with a grin.

"In a way, but we can't leave so much unspoken between us. It will be a wedge in our relationship, *jah*?"

"Agreed. Should I start then?"

She nodded.

"First off, I was a fool when I let my guard down with Hazel." He glanced at Martha, who was rigid, but listening intently. "I have absolutely no feelings towards the girl and I was just caught up in the moment. I'll forever regret what happened. It's no excuse to say I was lonely—though I was, and I can't blame her for what happened, though believe me, she did everything she could to make it happen. Anyway, I will always be faithful to you if you will come back to me. Always. Under any and all circumstances. My heart has never been anyone's but yours. I just want you to give me another chance."

"*Jah*, I believe you mean it, Paul. It's taken a while for me to forgive, and I'm sorry for not talking to you when you came by before, but I wasn't ready then. I hope you understand."

"Of course, I do. You had every right to be upset with me. I shouldn't have just popped in on you like that. I'm sorry. It wasn't fair."

"And I should have allowed you to stay, but what's done, is done. Are you finished yet?"

He chuckled. "Not completely, Martha. I want to say this. I've been selfish not to understand your need to be here to take care of your *mamm*. She needs you at this time. I hope it wasn't jealousy on my part. I'm afraid I kind of wanted you all to myself, and that was wrong and childish. I'm proud of the way you show your love and loyalty to your folks, and I hope you can all forgive me for pressuring you like I did."

"It's okay. I understand. Are you finished yet?"

He laughed and patted her hand. "Goodness, you seem in a rush."

She shook her head. "No, you finish what you have to say, then you can hear me out."

"Well, I'm going to leave my business with Jeremiah and come here to live. I actually already contacted a furniture maker in Lancaster and they said they could use another hand."

"No, you can't do that."

"Shhh. Listen now. Nothing is that important. I'll save for another house. I think Ben is interested in buying out my share of the business. If it doesn't work out with him, Jeremiah could pay me back slowly for what I've invested. A *gut* carpenter can always make a *gut* living. Eventually, I'll try to start my own place, but in the meantime, I'll be making a decent living."

"The house we were going to live in—you've put so much time into it."

"It's just a house. We can build our own someday. Maybe we can live with your folks for a year or so while we build something. As the *boppli* arrive, we can add rooms or a wing."

"Paul, I can't believe you'd do all that for me."

"Honey, I would do just about anything for you. The only thing I can think of that I wouldn't do, is deny Jesus. That will never happen."

"Oh, and it shouldn't! Ever! He must always be first in our lives, Paul."

He nodded and then reached over to hold her close again. She raised her lips to his and they kissed. It was a special moment that would remain in their memories for their lifetimes.

"Now," she said, moving back slightly. "You must hear what I have to say."

"You have my full attention, sweet Martha."

"My mother sat me down just the other day and told me that she wants me to move to your home if we marry. She's real insistent. She's felt guilty for expecting me to remain nearby, even though I've wanted to. She's not going to take no for an answer."

"But…your place is here. I realize that now. And what if the cancer isn't gone when they test her?"

"She has no fear of death. She told me my happiness comes first, and my *daed* will be there for her, no matter what the outcome."

Paul shook his head. "I can't tell you how much it means to me to have her say these things, and I'm sure she means every word, but I see things with new eyes, Martha, and I believe we need to be here, no matter what the results. You have your *daed* to think about and your grandparents. Also, your *Aenti* Lizzy, who loves you like you're her own *dochder*. If we marry, you must listen to your husband, *jah*?"

"Well, we're not married yet," she said, smiling over.

"I can move over here right away and get a room somewhere. Maybe I can rent a room from your *aenti* and pay them for room and board till we marry. That way I can go with you to your Bishop and learn about your *Ordnung* while you're preparing for baptism. It makes sense to me. I think I could start work right away in Lancaster. The boss said one of his employees lives only a mile from here. He's a Mennonite and drives his own car. He's sure he could pick me up every day. It's all lining up, Martha. I believe it's what *Gott* would want us to do. Things were terrible between us when I was insisting on getting my way. Now, things are turning around completely. I'm much closer to *Gott* now, too. I'd come to depend on myself way too much."

"I will listen to you, Paul. If this is what *Gott* wants for us, who am I to argue with Him?"

"Or me!" Paul said as he kissed her on the tip of her nose.

"We can visit with the bishop tomorrow," Martha said. "Maybe we can set the date. The fall isn't that far away."

"My darling *maed*. You are the love of my life. My bride-to-be. May *Gott* always shed His grace on us."

"*Jah*, forever and ever."

* * * * *

Hope you are enjoying this series.
For more information please visit
the author's web page:
www.junebelfie.com

*Could this bad-boy newcomer spell trouble for an Amish
spinster...or be the answer to her prayers?*

*Read on for a sneak preview of
An Unlikely Amish Match,
the next book in Vannetta Chapman's miniseries
Indiana Amish Brides.*

The sun was low in the western sky by the time Micah Fisher
hitched a ride to the edge of town. The driver let him out at a dirt
road that led to several Amish farms. He'd never been to visit
his grandparents in Indiana before. They always came to Maine.
But he had no trouble finding their place.

As he drew close to the lane that led to the farmhouse, he
noticed a young woman standing by the mailbox. A little girl was
holding her hand and another was hopping up and down. They
were all staring at him.

"Howdy," he said.

The woman only nodded, but the two girls whispered, "Hello."

"Can we help you?" the woman asked. "Are you...lost?"

"*Nein.* At least I don't think I am."

"You must be if you're here. This is the end of the road."

Micah pointed to the farm next door. "Abigail and John Fisher
live there?"

"They do."

"Then I'm not lost." He snatched off his baseball cap, rubbed
the top of his head and then yanked the cap back on.

Micah stepped forward and held out his hand. "I'm Micah—
Micah Fisher. Pleased to meet you."

"You're not *Englisch*?"

"Of course I'm not."

"So you're Amish?" She stared pointedly at his clothing—tennis shoes, blue jeans, T-shirt and baseball cap. Pretty much what he wore every day.

"I'm as Plain and simple as they come."

"I somehow doubt that."

"Since we're going to be neighbors, I suppose I should know your name."

"Neighbors?"

"*Ja.* I've come to live with my *daddi* and *mammi*—at least for a few months. My parents think it will straighten me out." He peered down the lane. "I thought the bishop lived next door."

"He does."

"Oh. You're the bishop's *doschder*?"

"We all are," the little girl with freckles cried. "I'm Sharon and that's Shiloh and that is Susannah."

"Nice to meet you, Sharon and Shiloh and Susannah."

Sharon lost interest and squatted to pick up some of the rocks. Shiloh hid behind her *schweschder*'s skirt, and Susannah scowled at him.

"I knew the bishop lived next door, but no one told me he had such pretty *doschdern*."

Susannah's eyes widened even more, but it was Shiloh who said, "He just called you pretty."

"Actually I called you all pretty."

Shiloh ducked back behind Susannah.

Susannah narrowed her eyes as if she was squinting into the sun, only she wasn't. "Do you talk to every girl you meet that way?"

"Not all of them—no."

Don't miss
An Unlikely Amish Match *by Vannetta Chapman,*
available February 2020 wherever
Love Inspired® *books and ebooks are sold.*

LoveInspired.com

SPECIAL EXCERPT FROM

Love Inspired®
SUSPENSE

On the run from Witness Protection, Iris James can only
depend on herself to stay alive...until a man she thought
was dead shows up to bring her back.

Read on for a sneak preview of
Runaway Witness *by Maggie K. Black, available in
February 2020 from Love Inspired Suspense.*

Iris James's hands shook as she piled dirty dishes high on
her tray. Something about the bearded man in the corner
booth was unsettlingly familiar. He'd been nursing his
coffee way longer than anyone had any business loitering
around a highway diner in the middle of nowhere. But it
wasn't until she noticed the telltale lump of a gun hidden
underneath his jacket that she realized he might be there
to kill her.

She put the tray of dirty dishes down and slid her hand
deep into the pocket of her waitress's uniform, feeling for
the small handgun tucked behind her order pad.

Iris stepped behind an empty table and watched the
man out of the corner of her eye. He seemed to avert his
gaze when she glanced in his direction.

A shiver ran down her spine. As if sensing her eyes on
him, the bearded man glanced up, and for a fraction of a
second she caught sight of a pair of piercing blue eyes.

Mack?

Mack's body had been found floating in Lake Ontario eight weeks ago with two bullets in his back. This man was at least ten pounds lighter than Mack, with a nose that was much wider and a chin a lot squarer.

She glanced back at the bearded man in the booth.

He was gone.

She pushed through the back door and scanned her surroundings. Not a person in sight.

She ran for the tree line and then through the snow-covered woods until she reached the abandoned gas station where she'd parked her big black truck.

Almost there. All she had to do was make it across the parking lot, get to her camper, leap inside and hit the road.

The bearded man stepped out from behind the gas station.

She stopped short, yanked the small handgun from her pocket and pointed it at him with both hands. "Whoever you are, get down! Now!"

Don't miss
Runaway Witness *by Maggie K. Black,*
available February 2020 wherever
Love Inspired® Suspense books and ebooks are sold.

LoveInspired.com

LOVE INSPIRED

INSPIRATIONAL ROMANCE

UPLIFTING STORIES OF FAITH, FORGIVENESS AND HOPE.

———————

Join our social communities to connect with other readers who share your love!

Sign up for the Love Inspired newsletter at **LoveInspired.com** to be the first to find out about upcoming titles, special promotions and exclusive content.

———————

CONNECT WITH US AT:

Facebook.com/LoveInspiredBooks

Twitter.com/LoveInspiredBks

Facebook.com/groups/HarlequinConnection

Looking for more satisfying love stories
with community and family at their core?

Check out **Harlequin® Special Edition**
and **Love Inspired®** books!

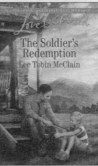

New books available every month!

CONNECT WITH US AT:

Facebook.com/groups/HarlequinConnection

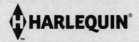

Facebook.com/HarlequinBooks

Twitter.com/HarlequinBooks

Instagram.com/HarlequinBooks

Pinterest.com/HarlequinBooks

ReaderService.com

HARLEQUIN®

**ROMANCE WHEN
YOU NEED IT**

HFGENRE2018

Love Harlequin romance?

DISCOVER.

Be the first to find out about promotions, news and exclusive content!

Facebook.com/HarlequinBooks

Twitter.com/HarlequinBooks

Instagram.com/HarlequinBooks

Pinterest.com/HarlequinBooks

ReaderService.com

EXPLORE.

Sign up for the Harlequin e-newsletter and download a free book from any series at **TryHarlequin.com**

CONNECT.

Join our Harlequin community to share your thoughts and connect with other romance readers!
Facebook.com/groups/HarlequinConnection

HARLEQUIN

HSOCIAL2020